SHORT STORIES III

from

The BookMark Shoppe

10 9 8 7 6 5 4 3 2 1

First Edition, October 2016

Published in the United States, by

The BookMark Shoppe

Cover Design & Layout by Christine Freglette

Edited by Lisa Cappiello

Table of Contents

ROSA
Johanna Dehler

Once again, Frau Plattner made me work until 10:00 p.m. Sure, I am the apprentice who does the best job in her shop, she says. My eyes sting from focusing on the tiny stitches. Because Frau Hofrat needs her evening gown ready for her fitting tomorrow. She is supposed to go to the opening of Goethe's Faust at the Landestheater on the weekend. Of course, we made sure the dress' cut and the fabric are as flattering as possible. So tomorrow, I'll be at work by 7:00 a.m. to clean up the place so Frau Hofrat can have her fitting at 9. Frau Plattner always makes me work late – and then consoles me with sweet words – like I'm the best, the most reliable, blah, blah, blah. What Frau Plattner and Frau Hofrat do not know is that I will actually be at the opening night of Faust as well. Yes, I will be up in the nosebleed seats – I got my ticket for 3 Schilling and 50 Groschen. I'll be wearing my black suit that I made to attend Klara's wedding. It's not Frau Hofrat's evening gown but what do I care. I have read Faust from front to back at least three times. Not the reading they assign me at trade school!

***

The curtain closes. Intermission time. The theater is buzzing with voices. The ladies in their boxes get up or move their chairs to show off their gowns and jewels. Manfred Oderdonk as Mephisto is divine! And how about the set design! Quite daring to go so minimalistic in the second act! Rosa's heart is beating. She just loves getting lost in the rhythm of the language. She even remembers a few of the rhyming couplets she has learned by heart. She and her friend Hetty also get up and walk down the stairs, lushly covered with red carpet, to the foyer where the theater guests mingle. Some have purchased champagne and salute each other with their champagne flutes. What a splendid performance! Rosa and Hetty can't afford champagne, of course. Even the Mineralwasser is too expensive for them. But they chat and watch the illustrious guests in their gowns and dapper suits walk by. Aaaah, Frau Hofrat is here. Her plump figure looks much slimmer in the black and golden gown. Rosa certainly picked a good cut. Frau Hofrat sees Rosa but looks through her as if she didn't exist. Who's Rosa anyway, that scrawny little girl from the dressmaker's shop? Rosa feels a stab of pain in her chest. It hurts to be ignored. After she spent hours – days! – cutting the dress, sewing it, fitting it. Rosa watches herself in disbelief as the words just slip out, "Oh, Frau Hofrat! How wonderful to see you! You look splendid in that dress! And what an amazing performance, isn't it?" Frau Hofrat turns red as a beet and turns abruptly around. Rosa crossed the line. The little seamstress dared to speak. Frau Plattner will be furious.

***

The sun was up. It was a glorious morning, the mountains with their white snow caps outlined against a deep blue spring sky. The trees' light green foliage reflected in the sunlight. As usual, Rosa had taken the bike to get to work. She loved pedaling really fast, right behind the red street cars. Weeeh – Rosa took a corner, and another. Now it got a little wobbly over the cobblestones. She entered Maria-Theresien-Strasse, one of the fanciest shopping streets in town. Shop windows tastefully displayed clothing and shoes; there was an antique shop specializing in engravings and a fancy pastry shop where tables and chairs were set up on the sidewalk. Rosa is almost there - Frau Plattner's salon. She gets off her bike, pushes it inside the corridor and locks it. She walks up the wide stairway (marble) to the first floor where a polished brass plate advertises: "Margarethe Plattner. Feine Damenmode." Fine Ladies Fashion. She walked in – Hetty was already there and a few other girls. Frau Plattner herself usually showed up at 8:30 a.m. Hetty and Rosa started laughing when they see each other. Even though they know Rosa had crossed a line, Frau Hofrat's red face was just too funny . . . ."You know I can get cheap tickets for next week's Mozart concert at the Hofgarten," Hetty said. "I know the guy who sells the tickets and he owes me a favor." "Maybe Herr Joachim will be there?" Hetty asked with a twinkle in her eye. Herr Joachim was a boarder who rented a room across Rosa's family's apartment. Renting this room to students contributed to the modest family income. Rosa liked Herr Joachim. He was so polite, so calm. He was a hard worker, too. A chemistry student, he could be seen on his bike at 6:30

in the morning to get to the laboratory to work on his experiments. He had started working on his dissertation – and there were many experiments to be completed. But what Rosa really loved about Herr Joachim was his ability to play the piano. He played Beethoven's Pathetique and Chopin's Raindrop Prelude. Herr Joachim practiced piano at the house of two eccentric twin sisters who had stayed unmarried and had been living in a picturesque little villa they inherited from their father. If Rosa had time, she sometimes stopped at the twin

sisters' house on Thursday night –
when Herr Joachim would play and
the sisters prepared a simple
dinner. Listening to music, like
reading literature and going to the
theater, opened Rosa's confined,
small world. She was transposed
into an enchanting realm of beauty,
beyond the daily struggles of
making ends meet.

***

Frau Plattner raised her
meticulously plucked arched
eyebrows. "So, it has come to my
attention that you have been going
out with Herr Joachim …. to
concerts …. and such. That's … um

.... nice." She forced a smile on her lips that could not hide her surprise and disapproval. It was no secret that Frau Plattner felt that her own daughters should be going out with someone like Herr Joachim – "ein angehender Akademiker" (a future academic). The class lines were drawn pretty rigidly. But Rosa didn't care about class. She cared about beauty. She cared about inspiration. She cared about that moment when her soul took flight when she looked at a painting or listened to a spellbinding passage in a symphony. As her mind started to soar, she felt happy. Sure, it would be nice not having to worry about every Groschen, but she was practical-minded and knew how to make that particular Groschen stretch for a while. Being an apprentice at a dressmaker's was of course not the path for "höhere Töchter" – the higher daughters of society who were trained to be the wives of the future doctors and lawyers. A school for "höhere Töchter" had a curriculum that combined the arts -- literature, music, drawing/painting – with some practical topics, including home economics to run a proper high bourgeois household and cooking – appropriate for their elevated station in life, of course. It included an induction into the Austrian culinary arts – Tafelspitz,* Sachertorte,* Salzburger Nockerl* and the whole breadth of tasty, but time consuming and exacting recipes. Rosa learned to cook at her mom's house, mostly by helping out at an early age. She sure knew how to prepare a few yummy dishes, her Rollbraten* in particular, was quite mouthwatering. But it was not the Höhere Töchter curriculum that

---

* Tafelspitz is tender beef, boiled in broth; Sachertorte a classic chocolate cake; Salzburger Nockerl a sweet soufflé, and Rollbraten a rolled pork roast.

girls like Heidi Obermeier (one of the local doctor's daughters) learned. Yet, Rosa had her pride. She knew she was a good and smart worker – and she had her dreams. With ardent enthusiasm, she soaked up what was around her. She had a few poetry books, including one by Georg Trakl. They didn't have music records or a turntable at home, but they had a radio and Rosa often had to fight her sister Berta when she wanted to listen to classical music while Berta wanted to hear the latest foxtrott. Hetty had a little turntable at her house, and Rosa and Hetty loved going to the local record store during their lunch break. They would walk down Maria-Theresien-Strasse arm in arm, two pretty young girls with their hair stylishly short and wearing A-line skirts like the pictures in the magazines. At home at Hetty's, they would drink tea from dainty china cups and listen to recordings by Yehudi Menuhin and Wilhelm Kempff.

***

In her wedding pictures, her dark hair framed her face in beautiful contrast to her dress, which was made of pale pink, hand-made lace. A simple, tailored cut, no ruffles or other frufru. A coat with three quarter sleeves, in pink a couple of shades darker than the dress and one tasteful decorative button was worn over it. The ensemble was completed with white long gloves and a pillbox hat - very Jackie O. - in the same lace fabric as the dress. Classy and unconventional. No white poofy dress for Rosa. Instead she made her own creation in her namesake color, "rosa." Pale pink roses with feathery ferns made up the bridal bouquet. Joachim was wearing a sharp suit with narrow lapels and a thin, silver tie with an abstract pattern. Everyone was there. Her sister Berta, with her hair in a classic 60s beehive; her niece Lilly, with a blond ponytail and her pretty dimpled face; her nephew Heinz, with freckles and a boyish smile; her brother-in-law, nicknamed "Grosser Heinz" ("big Heinz"), with long sideburns. Her older sister Anni and her husband Sepp (sporting a suave mustache) and their two kids, Klaus, blond and shy, and Christine, the oldest, looking at the camera with a mature and steady gaze. Rosa's mother, in a dark teal dress and a matching hat and veil, and Herr Vesper, with his bushy eyebrows and sparkly dark brown eyes, as usual dressed to the nines in a pin-striped suit and a bow tie, holding a John Player Special cigarette. And, of course, her friend Hetty, in a little black dress and pearls, very Parisian. They toasted with South Tyrolean wine to a long and happy life.

***

Rosa and Joachim walked to their usual balcony seats in the concert hall. It wasn't too crowded there, and, according to Joachim, had the best acoustics. Over all this time, going to concerts continued to be one of their favorite things to do together. Now, as they were about to enter their golden years, they no longer had to skimp to get decent tickets. Rosa was wearing a navy suit (as usual, impeccably tailored) with a yellow silk blouse. Joachim's dark navy suit matched hers, with an amber, paisley-patterned tie that Rosa picked out. They nodded their hellos, as other couples entered, some of their neighbors, some of Joachim's co-workers, their daughter's piano teacher. Ah, and here was the Mayor and his wife, and a few City Council members. "So, the haute volée has arrived." An almost imperceptible ironic smile played on Joachim's lips. Rosa returned the smile, just as subtle.

The orchestra started tuning their instruments. A buzzing cloud of sound, full of anticipation. The high notes of the violins, flutes, and clarinets fused with the lower vibrato of the chellos and the soft sounds of the timbals. Slowly the lights dimmed. The main spotlight was on the large, shiny black piano. It was open to expose its golden interior, displaying its intricate mechanics and strings. There was a hush as the conductor walked out, shook the first violinist's hand and took his place at the podium. He turned to his left, with a welcoming gesture to the pianist. Dressed in a black tailcoat, he took a deep bow as the audience clapped. The conductor raised his baton. A golden, magic moment of silence. Rosa held Joachim's hand. He looked at her, with his gentle eyes. The orchestra played the opening chord, and Daniel Barenboim's fingers touched the keys to strike the beginning notes of Beethoven's 5th piano concerto.

A Lyly Beneath the Tree
Vanessa Laureano Acosta

Evangelina sat in the bathroom
with her face in her hands as the
noises from a full house came
muffled through the door. As she
sat on the bathroom floor,
flashbacks of her beloved mother
came to her. The never ending
tears rolled down her cheeks. How
did she get here and what would
she do now? Her small, fishbowl of
a life had been overturned and she
wondered what she would do now
with her time. She had dedicated
most of her time to caring for her
mother that she became her world,

her existence. The small bathroom had become her refuge and as she heard the familiar voices of her sister, nephew, daughter, and husband, she gathered herself, wiped the tears, looked and asked God words that would not only haunt her, but would give her the strength she needed for the days ahead, "God make me numb."

The funeral parlor was bleak and cold. I remember the distant memory of visiting this dark place. A place that did not seem to fit into my life. I remember looking at my sister, Grace when we got there and the same question kept coming back, 'how did we get here?' I thought the selecting of the coffin and the clothes were bad, but picturing my mom just lying there did not seem real and fair. As I took the few steps to enter the room that my mother was going to be viewed in, I thought to myself that we had just spoken two days ago, and we had made plans to cook dinner together, but now no dinner would ever be made and no more dreams or memories would be made either. I entered, stopped, took a deep breath, and became numb.

The funeral, like most, was sad, but in true fashion to my mother's testimony, there was a sense of rejoicing and celebration. I finally took a moment and sat down and looked around the room. I saw many faces and for that one moment, I felt happiness and peace. Happy that my mom had touched so many lives. I closed my eyes and a distant but vivid memory came to me. I was no more than a seven year old little girl. I had just come out of the shower and was sitting on the edge of my mother's bed. I remember thinking how in awe I was of being in the room. The room looked larger than life. I smile and think I have always been in awe of her and I hope she knew that. I could smell my mother's favorite shampoo and conditioner, Wella Balsam, and then I felt what I was searching for, her touch, her closeness, her smell. She was combing my hair and the silent, distant sound of the blow dryer filled my head and out tunes the sniffles and cries of the mourners

that sat by me. It was a
silent memory of my mother
and we did not speak, but amazing
things happen in silence
sometimes. Who would have
thought that a memory that seemed
so ordinary would be so very
important later on in life?

Through the constant multitude of
people who were there hugging,
kissing, and giving meaningful
words to us and the others in
attendance, memories kept flooding
back in a tsunami of waves. As I

stared at her body, I felt the summer sun on my face. It was two days after giving birth to my daughter and my mother and I were walking back to the apartment. The summer morning breeze moved through us and I remembered the sky being a beautiful clear shade of blue with spots of white clouds floating by us. There was no noise on the streets, just the chirping of the birds on this early Saturday morning. My mother held me by the elbow leading the way as we walked in silence the two blocks to my apartment. Leading as she always did, guiding me in the right direction, opening my eyes to the possibilities of my talents and my dreams. I looked at her and we both smiled and then I looked again and I saw her laying in the coffin. How did I get here?

The room was full of people, there were so many that they were spilling out in the hallway of the funeral home and there was a mixture of people from the old to the young. It is said and believed that God does not allow you to get a glimpse of earth once you are in his presence, but I hope that for this once, he would have allowed you to see the number of people you touched and the impact you had on everyone. From your kind and loving words to your stern but influential advice,

your sternness was rare and infrequent, but in the end, your words were well intentioned, and very much treasured and appreciated. As I walked around in a haze, I made small talk with those in attendance. I heard words that floated by me saying she was and will be adored. I remember her constant words of affection. She felt your pain and happiness, but most importantly, how devoted she was.

When you spoke, your words were like honey, and people listened. God had given you many gifts, but your special gift of words hypnotized many. Proverbs 16:24 came to my mind as I sat there, "The speech of the wise is a honeycomb of honey, and it is sweet to his soul and healing to his bones." Oh how I could just hear you in the mist of all this noise. I closed my eyes and my memories took me to the very first day that you were released from the nursing facility after being away from us for so long and enduring what you did. You were finally back home with us. We had eight long months of not having you home and finally the day came. I saw myself kneeling at your legs and my head buried in your lap as I sobbed uncontrollably, tears of relief, of happiness, of finally being able to let go and not be the strong one anymore. The matriarch of the family, the substance of this family, was finally home. Your hand was stroking my hair and your sweet words were

telling me not to cry. Those words -
how I long to hear your advice, your
jokes, your love, because even in
your words there was love. Every
word had a meaning. You did not
speak to fill the room with words,
but you spoke to fill the hearts of
the many who came to you for
advice, or just to simply sit by you
and learn from you. How short
those moments would be as you
shortly died within a year.

I was brought back to reality as the
eulogy started and Grace, myself,

the children, and father sat in the front seats. Five pastors were situated in the front of the room beside where you lay and the smell of lavender touched my senses. How fitting that you smelt like lavender as your favorite color was purple. You were dressed beautifully, your hair was up in a bun (your natural look), and your nails were painted in that soft color rose you liked as well. I smiled and recalled telling you as you prepared for your wedding day that I was not going to look like Barney and refused to wear purple. So because of your loving heart, I wore white

just like you, and you were so proud
that I looked like you. It was your
day and you did not even care to
share your moment. As I
hear stories and testimonies of the
great life you lived in helping
people, I hope that you knew how
much you mattered and that life
without you will be a void in a lot of
people's lives.

The singing and the testimonies
continued and I knew that the night
was coming to an end, and that
tomorrow would be, by far, the

hardest day of my life. As the mourners left and it dwindled down to the immediate family, I found myself doing my nightly routine to make sure my mother was okay for the night. How funny to continue with something that holds not so much significance anymore. I was the last one in the room and I went to kiss your forehead and say "bendicion." As I left the room, my heart and soul crumpled. The rest of the night was a blur, but I do remember crawling in bed with Grace and just letting her hold me like when I was a little girl in Puerto Rico. I am so happy that I have

Grace to hold on to, to be able to share all my memories, all my longings with.

Morning came too quickly and my last day with my mother approached. Everything was done in a fog. I dressed myself and then Marita, my beautiful daughter. I wondered how the kids were holding up as they were my mother's pride and joy and for Marita, my mother was her second mother and friend. I am comforted that they got to meet, that she made an impact in her life, and that she learned from her as well. They will always have memories, and many of them were filled with laughter. Walking in to find my mother who had just come home from the nursing home dancing in the living room with Marita and my nephew as she was still attached to the oxygen machine will always be one of the happiest times that I cherish. Their laughter resonating throughout the living room and the smiles on the kids' faces made me appreciate her even more for she made them happy, and they made her happy, and they made her feel alive once again.

We arrived at the funeral home on a cold, windy January morning. It was quiet and as we said our final goodbyes, the heaviness in the air was felt by many. One by one my family entered the room and silently said their goodbyes. I didn't leave and stayed behind with the pallbearers. I leaned against the doorframe hoping that it would hold me up and I watched as the lid was closed. It would be, for some, closure, but for me, it was only the beginning. The rebirth of a new world where there would be no direction, no more of the warmth of the loving arms of a mother. I now know the meaning of being empty and numb. I walked outside and found that there was no room for me in any of the cars and the only room was in the hearse. I opened the door to the hearse, sat, and looked ahead. Once again, the smell of lavender engulfed me and I just bowed my head and smiled as a single tear rolled down my cheek. Till the very end I promised that I would take care of you, and, sitting in that hearse, I completed my promise.

The drive to the cemetery was filled with sharing memories with the driver, and talking about the kind of women my mother was, and how she will be so missed. How proud I was in speaking of you. When I finally looked up, I saw the cemetery, and the dread I felt when I saw you that first day when you died crept back up. We arrived and the crisp, cold air hit me, but I was so numb that not even that would break me.

They buried you under a tree
the way you always wanted and
doves made a nest on the branch
directly above you. We visit you
though we know that you are no
longer there, but you are still my
mother, and stories still need to be
told. It's been five very long and
hard years without you, and a new
family member has joined us. Our
precious Lilia, who is so much like
you, and she finally makes our
hearts sing and smile. As I prepared
to write about who you were, so
that she may know you the way we
all did, I thanked God for giving me

the opportunity to have met you and to have had the privilege of calling you my mother. I am no longer numb, I am alive. I am finally at peace because every time I see her smile, every time I hear someone tell me that there is something about her that calls them to her, I smile and know that God placed her in our lives to fill the void that you left. Thank you, for I am who you raised me to be. I am you.

Abduction

Ellen O'Rourke-Dominianni

He couldn't take his eyes off
her. He watched her exit the
minivan and walk around to the
passenger side to retrieve her
purse, all the while talking into her
cell phone. As she walked into
Starbucks, she tilted her head to
hold the phone so she could carry
her bag with two hands, just like his
mother used to. She was striking.
Her shoulder length blonde curls
and ocean blue eyes reminded him
of his mother. He got another cup
of coffee so he could pass the table
where she and her black-haired

friend were sitting. Around her neck was a large heart-shaped gold pendant with a picture of a little girl and boy with the same blond curls. Her white scrubs had her name, Ashley Jones RN, embroidered above her heart. "I'm sorry I was late, Lisa," he overheard her say. "Work was crazy." Her companion said something he couldn't hear because his heart was beating so loud and he was breathing so heavily. His search was over! He went into overdrive, planning his next move.

She and her friend sat talking for a while after they finished their coffee. He was too far away to hear their conversation. Just when he was starting to think they would never leave, he noticed the other one start to pack up her stuff. He made himself invisible and left.

***

As usual, Ashley was late to pick up Haley and Drew. She hurriedly unlocked the Toyota and drove to the kids' school. They were sleepy and as soon as she drove away, she could hear them snoring. Dusk was falling, emphasizing the disrepair of the buildings around her. She hated this neighborhood. It was being taken over by druggies. She was lost in thought and never noticed the dirty white van pull up behind her. Suddenly she heard an engine rev and a muffled bump. Her car shot forward. She pressed harder on the brake and put the car into park. She opened the driver side door to check on the kids. As she did, she felt a rough cloth push into her face, forcing her head back against her headrest. For a split second she smelled something sweet and then everything went black.

***

He pulled up in front of the dilapidated, pale green house surrounded by a high wire fence with a padlock on the front gate. In the yard, the bare dirt floor was littered with dog feces and fast food wrappers. A dirty white pit bull jumped onto a black one and they tussled in the dirt for a minute. They were both chained to the fence behind the house. A cracked concrete path started at the gate and morphed into three warped steps leading up to the door. Exiting the front of the house and snaking down to the bottom of the steps was a rusted pipe railing. The ripped screen in the aluminum front door curled in toward the heavy wooden inner door.

When he was a kid, the block had been filled with families and children. He recalled playing stickball, street hockey and skelly with his friends. Now, his was the only house on the block that was still inhabited. The others were beautiful back in the day, but now their wraparound porches were falling apart. Most of the windows were boarded over, the rest gaping holes. The yellow house on the corner was a crack-house but, due to the cold and a recent

drug/prostitution crackdown, was
currently empty.

He glanced up and down the
block, elated to see that he was
alone. Even the drug dealers didn't
want to be out in this weather. He
unlocked the padlock, yelled at the
dogs to stop barking and left the
gate ajar. He drove Ashley's
minivan back to the garage. He
opened the garage door quickly,
and drove the minivan in, closing
the door behind him. When he
opened the door to the van he was
relieved to see that they were still
drugged. The woman was much
lighter than she looked and she was

still sleeping, but not as deeply as before. He took care of the kids first and then cut the plastic ties on her wrists and ankles and placed her on the bed.

***

Ashley awoke to the sound of a TV blaring. As she sat up, she realized her hands and feet hurt like they had been bound.   Her mouth was dry and she had a dull headache. The musty smell of the room triggered her memory of the rough cloth in her face and the sweet smell.   *This is not my house!* she thought. *Where am I?* She looked around. *Haley! Drew! Where are they?* she thought, her breath coming in gasps as she remembered they were in the car with her when she was abducted.

She stood up quickly, wincing in pain. *What the hell?* There was something heavy and cold around her right ankle and it was digging into her skin. She looked down and saw that her ankle was manacled. A long chain went from her foot to a metal pole. She started to cry. "Hayley. Drew." She called out nervously. No answer. *Where were they?* She had to find them.

She looked around the room. There were two doors. One was

closed. The other was open and she could see what looked like a hallway. Quietly, she walked toward the open door, the chain dragging loudly behind her. Slowly, to minimize the noise, she walked into the hallway and saw a faded pink room to the right. Amid a vast array of Barbie dolls and accessories, she saw Haley's curly blonde hair. As she made her way to the bed, she noted that Haley's breathing was rhythmic and shallow. She was asleep. Whoever took them had drugged her but Ashley was relieved to find that Haley's heart rate and respirations were low but normal. Her right foot was also manacled and attached to a chain. To Ashley's right was a console TV which was the source of the noise. Afraid to attract the attention of whoever kidnapped them, Ashley left the TV alone and quietly made her way to the room across the hall.

This room was painted a faded royal blue. She spotted Drew sleeping soundly on a red racing car shaped bed with Hot Wheels linens. Like Haley, he was sleeping and had been drugged. His right foot was also chained to a pole to the left of the doorway.

Quickly, she checked the third open door which revealed a bathroom. She made her way back to the rooms that held her children. One by one she carried them into the room she woke up in. She was grateful the chains were long enough.

Now that she had eyes on them, she looked around at the room. It was windowless and dark; the only light came from a small lamp sitting on a nightstand in the corner next to the open door. The bed was an old fashioned double bed with matching flowered sheets, pillow cases and comforter. There was a small table with four chairs around it near the closed door. Above the table was a clock. It had birds instead of numbers and, Ashley would learn later, played bird sounds on the hour. All the furniture was old fashioned and made of wood, probably cherry. It looked pretty old. The chain attached to her ankle terminated in a large pile at the bottom of a thick metal pole which stood between the bed and the table. The ornate headboard was against the wall and the left side of the bed was against the perpendicular wall. Two large wooden closets faced the bottom of the bed.

She opened one of the wooden closets and found drawers full of women's clothes. They too were dated. She looked through the drawers for a weapon but came up empty. She checked the other closet and it was also full of clothes in drawers.   She pulled on the bottom drawer but it refused to open. After a few yanks, the whole drawer came out. With it came a small, wrinkled photo.

She scooped the clothes back into the drawer and put it back where it belonged. She unfolded the photo and saw that it was a picture of a man, a woman and two children. The man was smiling but everyone else looked scared. The man did not look familiar but the woman and children did.

Ashley's mind reeled. She remembered seeing pictures on the news of the same woman and children. Valerie Martinez, her son Juan and daughter Maria had been missing for a year. Valerie's husband had been arrested, but released after no evidence was found against him. But Nancy Grace had tried and convicted him in the media. Even Ashley had believed he killed them.

Last week had been the anniversary of their disappearance. There was so much news coverage that Ashley and Lisa discussed it.

He had Valerie and her kids for a year! Where are they now? Ashley shuddered. *I have to think of a way to get us out of here as quickly as possible.* She stuck the picture back under the drawer and climbed into bed with her kids. She held them close to her as she tried to think of a way out.

***

He put his coat on and went through the back door into the garage. Pressing the key fob, he watched the doors to Ashley's minivan slide open. From the freezer chest next to the minivan, he picked up Juan's body. Carefully, he placed it in the seat behind the driver's seat and buckled the seatbelt. He had a hard time because the body was frozen. It did not fit in the seat the way a live person would. Next, he placed Maria's body in the seat next to Juan's and buckled her in. Closing the side doors, he opened the hatchback, and laid Valerie's body across the bottom of the car. After backing the minivan out of the garage, he padlocked the heavy door.

He drove the minivan to Union and Bond Streets, making a left on Bond and then a right onto Sackett Street. The dead-end street was isolated between two tall factory/warehouse buildings and totally deserted. Carefully, he placed Valerie's body in the driver's seat and buckled her in. After placing rolled up newspapers into the openings of the three full gas containers he had placed in the minivan earlier, he set fire to the newspapers. As he ran away, he heard the explosion.

***

Crap. I fell asleep, thought Ashley. Haley and Drew were stirring and she was glad that whatever he had given them was wearing off. She looked around the room and saw that a slip of paper had been slipped under the locked door. She extricated herself from the kids and their chains and picked it up. "Darling, I am so glad you and the children are home safely. I am preparing one of your favorite meals.   Please have the children dressed for dinner and wear the blue dress. Dinner will be at 6:00 P.M." She glanced at the wall clock which said 5:30. *Great. Kidnapped by a psycho and now he wants to play games.*

As she looked through the wardrobes for a blue dress, she mentally prepared herself for dinner. *At least I will see what I'm up against.* She quickly changed and calmly woke up the kids. "We have to play a pretend game," she told them. "We have to pretend that a stranger is Daddy. I know this goes against everything I have ever taught you, but it is very important that we play this game, so the stranger will be happy and let us go home to your real Daddy."

"I'm scared Mommy," said Haley.

"Darling, you know how much Mommy and Daddy love you and I won't let anything happen to you. We can do this, okay?"

"Yes, Mommy." Haley still didn't look thrilled. Ashley hugged her and then hugged Drew.

"We can do this," Ashley said again, more to herself than the kids.

***

Downstairs, he listened to the sound of her footsteps mixed with the metal chain dragging across the parquet floor upstairs. In the quiet that followed, his mind overflowed with possibilities now that his "family" was complete. Again. This time everything would work out right. His wife loved him! After all, she had come back to him. He checked the clock; twenty minutes to six. Time to get ready.

***

Ashley and the kids sat at the table at five to six. "Okay, remember: act like he is Daddy."

"Do we have to kiss him?"

"No. If he tries to kiss you, I will say you have a sore throat."

*****

As he entered the room, Ashley did a quick assessment. She realized he was a few inches shorter than her. He had piercing blue eyes and sandy, blond curly hair with a slightly receding hairline. His shoulder length curls were pulled back into a short ponytail. He wore a fitted, black, short-sleeved button-down shirt and black silk Armani pants with black dress shoes. He was thin, but muscular. He did not look directly at Ashley and actually never made eye contact with her.

He wheeled in a cart covered with fresh fruit, salad, and several main dishes. From underneath, he pulled out dishes, glasses, napkins and silverware and passed them to Haley, who silently set the table. Ashley noticed that he did not make eye contact with the kids, either. Dinner consisted of a rotisserie chicken with sides of mashed potatoes and coleslaw.   They ate in silence, he ravenously and the rest of them just picking. When they were done, Ashley and Haley cleared the table onto the cart. Wordlessly, he took the cart and left.

"I don't like him, Mommy," Haley and Drew said in unison.

"That's good, but we have to play the game so we can get home to Daddy. Now it's time for bed," said Ashley.

"Can we sleep with you, Mommy?" asked Drew.

"Of course," said Ashley.

While the kids slept, Ashley got busy thinking of a plan to get away. He was shorter than her.

That was a definite advantage. But he was muscular and that was a disadvantage. As she dozed off, she played potential escape scenarios in her mind.

She woke with a start when the clock struck six. The kids were snoring lightly. There was a slip of paper on the floor near the door. She picked it up. "Dinner was lovely. See you at 8:00 A.M. for breakfast. Love, B." Ashley's skin crawled.

For the next two days, things continued in the same manner, notes before breakfast and dinner and meals eaten in silence. After their third dinner, Ashley got the kids ready for bed and put them in the other rooms to watch TV. She herself watched the news. A minivan with her license plates had been found burning near the Gowanus. There were three bodies inside and the reporter said the police refused to confirm or deny that they belonged to Ashley, Haley and Drew. The coroner was working on identifying them. Ashley thought of the photo of Valerie and her kids. *Who was in that van?* She knew she had to take action. She got the kids and they all slept together as they had every other night.

In the morning, she got up at 6:00 A.M. She chose her clothes: a pair of thin sweats with a tee shirt and sneakers. She helped the kids change into comfortable play clothes with sneakers and socks. Then she put on a pair of gloves and examined the long chain attached to her ankle. She worked with it a while until she was sure she could maneuver it the way she needed to.

At 7:30 A.M., Ashley spoke quietly with the children. She did not want to tell them what she was doing in case she had to change her plans, but she wanted them awake and alert enough to follow directions.

At 7:45 A.M, she had the kids go into the other room. She walked around trying not to appear nervous. She picked up the chain, looped it into her right hand and stood next to the door, keeping the chain in her right hand hidden behind the door. At 8:00 A.M., he unlocked and opened the door. As usual, he turned back to wheel in the tray. He was slightly bent over, facing the tray and while his back was turned, Ashley grabbed the chain with both hands and wrapped it, quickly and tightly, around his neck. She pulled as hard as she could, holding on for dear life. She climbed onto his back gripping and twisting the chain tighter as he tried to turn. He was unable to turn, however, due to her added weight and the way he was bent. After what seemed like an eternity, his legs collapsed under him. As he fell to the ground, Ashley pulled tighter. She held the chain tight for a full five minutes after he stopped moving, watching the wall clock upside down. The keys were in the door. Hurriedly, she found the key to the manacle and unlocked herself. She tied his hands with the tablecloth and dragged him over and wedged him under the bed. She was pretty sure he was dead but did not want to chance him coming to and going after her or the kids.

She ran to the other rooms and unlocked the kids' chains. "Hurry, we have to get out of here," she told them. As they ran through the bedroom, the kids eyed the body warily. "It's okay kids, he is sleeping now," she said. "Let's hurry."

When she got downstairs, she saw an old yellow phone hanging on the wall. She picked it up, doubtful it would work.   She heard a loud dial tone and quickly called 911, all the while watching the stairs (afraid he would come down). She whispered her name and said she had no idea where she was. "Oh my God," said the 911 operator Mary, "Are you and the kids okay? Everyone is looking for you." She kept Ashley on the line while she dispatched the police and ambulances to the address found in the computer. They arrived inside of three minutes and Mary stayed on the phone with Ashley the whole time.

Ashley opened the inside door and unlocked the shabby screen door. The sun was shining brightly and she heard dogs barking nearby. She sat on a faded yellow couch facing the door with both kids on her lap and the phone cradled on her shoulder. Mary reassured her that help was on the way. Ashley looked at the pictures on the wall in front of her. They were faded pictures of a striking blond couple with a boy and a girl. In the pictures all four of them were smiling. As she looked from the pictures on the left to the pictures on the right side of the wall, the children gradually aged from infancy to about 12 years old.

Just then, she heard sirens and looked out the door. A minute or two later, she saw police cars and ambulances pull up outside. She heard dogs barking. She watched as a tall, attractive young policeman used bolt cutters to cut a padlock off the gate outside. There was momentary hesitation on the part of the police and EMS as they got inside the fence. They were looking to Ashley's right, at something in the yard. Then she heard someone yell, "It's okay. The dogs are chained and can't reach the front of the house."

As police and EMS workers swarmed the house, Ashley held onto Drew and Haley for dear life. They were clinging to her just as tightly. Once EMS established that the three of them were okay, they checked the man upstairs. When Ashley heard them yell that he was dead, she burst into tears. She really never believed she could kill anyone. A policewoman had been facing Ashley and the kids, but looking at something behind them. When Ashley started crying, the young woman moved closer to her

and gestured to look behind her. As
Ashley turned around, the woman
said, "You shouldn't feel too bad
about him. There's no telling how
many lives you've saved." On the
wall facing her, Ashley saw some
newer pictures. At first glance, they
looked like another set of family
photos, arranged the same way as
the others. On closer inspection,
Ashley realized the only constant in
those pictures was the man
upstairs. The women and children
in those pictures weren't smiling
and there was only one picture of
each group. She was shocked to see
that there were 10 pictures, each

with a different woman, boy and girl. All the children appeared to be around the same age as Haley and Drew.

While Ashley was looking at the pictures, the policewoman's phone rang. She answered it, "Laura Daley." While she was on the phone, she held up one finger and maintained eye contact with Ashley. After listening for a few seconds she said "Thanks," and hung up. She moved to the last picture on the right and pointed. "The coroner just identified the burned bodies in your minivan as this woman, Valerie Martinez, and her children."

Murder in the Confessional

Tom O'Rourke

"Bless me Father, for I have sinned. . . . . " After quite a few minutes in the confessional, a loud series of BANG, BANG, BANG, was heard. Three shots from within the confessional and the penitent fell out of the confessional and landed in a bloody mess, on the church floor.

"How did Father Donato Beroni end up in prison? What do you mean he murdered someone in confession?" These were the questions his parishioners were asking. Detective Dennis Shanahan had the task of arresting his boyhood friend, Father Don, but was terribly upset by having to arrest a priest. In the ensuing interrogation, nothing could be learned about the details of the crime. Father Don insisted that he could not break the seal of confession.

Father Beroni was a priest for 20 years. When he was young he wanted to be a priest. The church ceremonials always fascinated him and he felt a strong desire to be the celebrant at the various clerical functions. He studied hard and was the altar boy for all the special liturgies. After graduation from high school he entered the seminary. The day before his ordination, his father was killed. He was caught in a crossfire in his neighborhood. The police said he was an innocent victim in the wrong place at the wrong time.

Father Beroni became a priest in the same diocese and then continued his studies to gain a doctorate in Psychology. In addition to his parochial duties, he worked with the homeless and the unemployed, and when possible, did prison work hoping to assist criminals, who had served their time, return to society and become good citizens. He enlisted many of the local companies to consider hiring the former convicts to enable them to start a new life.

One of his boyhood friends started a network marketing franchise and encouraged Father Beroni to set up his own franchise. As a local diocesan priest who was not required to take a vow of poverty, his bishop agreed to allow him to do this. He used the franchise business to assist the homeless and unemployed by having local companies sponsor them and thereby enable them to get started. The program worked so well that he began to consider getting the former convicts to start their own franchise. This took considerable time as there was reluctance on the part of the franchise headquarters as well as the local sponsoring companies to go along with this novel and potentially hazardous venture.

He decided to let this idea rest for a while since all his previous efforts were successful and he did not want to jeopardize their future. Now he was facing jail time for a crime he was accused of committing. His arresting officer and boyhood friend, Detective Dennis Shanahan, had been encouraging Father Don, as he called him, to tell him exactly what happened in the confessional, but he insisted on declaring that his paramount duty was to protect the seal of confession.

The injured man, unable to speak, had been rushed to the hospital's Intensive Care Unit. He had no identification on him and it was impossible to obtain fingerprints as his fingertips were all missing. In addition, they discovered that his body was severely scarred from apparent old wounds. Eventually, he was identified as William Negroni, a decorated Veteran of the Vietnam War. His missing fingertips and bodily scars were the result of serious torture by the Viet Cong. This information increased the pressure on Father Don to explain why he shot him. He refused to admit that he shot him or to reveal what took place in the confessional.

The emphasis in this case had now shifted away from Father Beroni and there was a serious investigation into the life of Marine Sargent William Negroni. The investigative trail led back from his honorable discharge from the

Marine Corps to his enlistment and his duty as a Marine in the Vietnam War. Uncovering his past revealed he had a rough childhood, growing up with an alcoholic mother and a father who was shot by a cop in a botched robbery. Young William soon became "Billy the Kid" as his delinquent friends called him. He was tough and always ready to battle it out with anyone who challenged him. There was a cop who interrupted him as he was about to hold up a liquor store. The cop realized he a was smart, determined (if belligerent), young man. The policeman was a former marine, who recognized that given the proper training, William could be a good marine and become a responsible citizen.

Becoming a marine had more appeal than going to jail, so he agreed to sign up. His experience at Paris Island demonstrated to him that he could handle tough requirements and he began to develop genuine friendships with his fellow trainees. The Vietnam War was already in full bloom when he finished his basic training. He was given his orders to ship out to the West Coast and in a couple of weeks found himself in the middle of the Vietnam War. As a tough kid growing up in a rough neighborhood in Brooklyn, he was quick to adapt to tough situations. He soon found himself defending himself and his buddies against the cruel Viet Cong. His commanding officer recognized that this tough kid from Brooklyn would take on any difficult assignment and be sure to survive. In a short time, he had proved his bravery and his ability to protect his fellow marines. In one brutal firefight, members of his company were pinned down by the enemy. He then made his way around to the rear of the enemy, opened up his automatic weapon, and fired grenades at them. He created such noise and explosive force that the Viet Cong returned fire anticipating a large force of men behind them. Sargent Willie shouted at his men to get back to camp as he kept up the firing. Ten men made it back to camp but Willie did not. He was captured and taken away. During his capture he was viciously treated. At one point he slipped away and stole food to give to his fellow prisoners. He was caught, and because of his crime, they cut off the tips of all his fingers and using hot iron batons, sealed the tips, so that he could use his hands for work they wanted him to perform. He was kept in prison for more than a year and during that time spent many days in solitary confinement. He was constantly being lashed and his torso was scarred - front and back.

Eventually he was freed and returned to the states. Although a hero by military standards, he was treated like a criminal as were so many returning veterans of the Viet Nam War were considered. He hid his medals and never talked about the war. He returned to his Brooklyn neighborhood which had dramatically changed. He soon realized, as a veteran he was not welcomed. This was the secondary shame of the war. He had difficulty finding work and even considered going back to a life of crime, but the preciousness of life prevented him from doing so. Unemployed and without shelter, he became one of the many homeless veterans living on the streets and under bridges and roadways. He wanted to find his way out of this life and even contemplated suicide. In one of his most depressing moments, he saw a truck going by with a sign indicating a homeless outreach program at a nearby church. It was at that church that he came across the name 'Father Donato Beroni.' He did not meet him but the name seemed familiar to him. The outreach program enabled him to have a meal and find out how to get employment. They gave him the name of a nearby church that had a shelter so he could have a bed for the night. That night, as he settled in, he searched his mind for the name Beroni. Suddenly, it came to him. When he was a boy, his father was involved in a neighborhood shootout and an innocent bystander was killed in the crossfire. That man's name was Beroni. Willie reflected on his childhood. He was baptized a Catholic but long since gave up on religion and religious rituals, yet there he was, sheltered in a church, and fed by a church related outreach program.

He decided he now needed to return to church. He was a little boy when he first made his confession but the words were coming back to him, "Bless me Father…," and he began to repeat this phrase over and over. He left the shelter each day but continued to return each night. He talked to those who worked at the shelter to seek work.

They suggested they could use some help at the shelter. It would not pay anything, but he could keep busy and develop cooking skills and maybe eventually find employment. He liked the idea and began to brighten up, as each day he was doing something worthwhile. He soon learned that cooking meals was something he could do and found satisfaction when he realized that the other homeless people enjoyed the meals he prepared. Now that he was comfortable at the shelter, he decided he would go to confession, and hoped to restore his life. He wanted to find out where this Father Beroni was and confess to him. Maybe Father Beroni wanted to know who killed his father.

That was how he ended up in Father Beroni's confessional. Now he was in the Intensive Care Unit at the hospital and Father Beroni was in jail.

Detective Shanahan was responsible for finding out how these two men ended up in this situation. Detective Dennis Shanahan grew up in the same neighborhood as Father Beroni. They were classmates in grammar school and high school and kept in touch over the years.

As young boys, Dennis and Donato spent a lot of time together. When Donato was not in Church, he and Dennis played touch football and softball, depending on the season. Dennis called Don, "Church Knees" because he would always stop in to Church, even when he was not involved in a service as an altar boy. Don told Dennis, "You better become a cop or else you will end up behind bars because of your careless attitude about what's right and wrong." When Don went to the seminary, after high school graduation, Dennis went on to college, to study law, and then at the same time, filed an application for police work. He finished his bachelor's degree and since he had not heard from the Police Department, continued on to law school. He finished law school about the same time as Father Don was ordained. They celebrated their achievements together and promised to work with each other whenever and wherever they could. The Police Department's request for new recruits came about that time and Dennis went off to the Police Academy. His first few years as a new police officer found him developing quite a career as a serious cop. He soon took the Detective exam and passed it with flying colors. He was subsequently assigned to the Special Crimes Division, which is how he ended up investigating this special crime involving his best friend and a hero veteran. The two men involved in this crime, the priest and the veteran, required Dennis to maximize his investigative skills to determine exactly what happened and why. As he began to analyze this particular case, he realized that at the moment, nothing made sense.

Why would a priest, a close friend, shoot a veteran, in a confessional? Dennis decided he would have to return to the scene of the crime and find out what clues might be there. It was the middle of the afternoon, when he arrived at the church. This church was built in the early years of the previous century when the desire to build cathedrals was in the hearts and souls of so many of the Irish and Italian immigrants, who were thankful to God for giving them the opportunity to be in this country. They worked hard and saved their money and when asked to contribute to build a Church, they wanted it to be a wonderful edifice to reflect their love of their God. As Dennis entered, he sensed the smell of incense from an earlier service. The church was now darkened, with only the sacristy area lighted and the steep stone columns grey with the years of burning candle smoke leaving its reminder of all who had lit a candle for Aunt Mary, Uncle Tony, a sick child, or a dying parent. The ancient wooden pews gave the visitor the sense of seriousness that only an old cathedral can give. Dennis was reminded of his early days, at

Sunday mass and his times of receiving the sacraments.

As he glanced over to the right, all the way up front, he spotted the confessional with its door in the middle for the priest, and the side sections with the dark brown curtains, providing privacy for the penitents. The church appeared empty but as he looked all around, he noticed a woman kneeling in the last pew, all the way over to the left. The dimly lit church and her dark coat made her practically invisible. As he made his way over to her, he noticed that she was pouring her rosary into her left hand and then opened a rosary pouch to put her beads away. As he approached her she said to him, "You look like the detective…" Before she could say anymore he interrupted her and said "I am Detective Shanahan. I am investigating the shooting that occurred here."

"How is Dear Father Beroni?" she asked. Snanahan said, "He is in jail, but he is doing well." "What about that fellow who was shot"? "He is still in a coma, but he is improving." "Oh thank God, for both of them. What about the other man who ran away?"

"What man?" Shanahan had not heard of anyone else there at that time.

"Ma'am, what is your name?"

"I am Mrs. Bronkowski."

"Mrs. Brownkowski, would you tell me what you mean about the other man." "Were you here that day?"

"Our police officers said there was no one else here that day."

"I come here every afternoon to say my rosary. I stay back here where it is quiet. I don't like crowds or excitement."

"Did you hear the shots?"

"I did not hear anything. I have troubling hearing which is okay for me, because I don't have to listen to people gossip and talk about other people."

"Did you see anything that day"?

"I was finishing my rosary and as I looked up, I saw Fr. Beroni rush out of the confessional and run to the side. I saw the man on the other side run out and throw something towards Fr. Beroni. He then ran out that side door near the confessional. I left out this way, because I don't like crowds and I thought there might be people with uniforms coming. In my country (her heavy accent was beginning to show in her voice), when men in uniforms and guns appear, people get injured. I have not been back here until today."

"Mrs. Brownkowski, you have been very helpful. You have given me information that we did not have. If I asked you to describe the man you saw, would you be able to give me a description?"

"The only thing I can tell you is he looked like a homeless man, kind of sloppy, not very neat, about the same size as Fr. Beroni."

"If we had our sketch artist see you, would you be able to describe this person in more detail?"

"I'm sorry Detective, but I have given you the best description I can."

"Thank you for all your help. Here is my card. Please call me if you think of anything else that might help us."

After leaving the church, Shanahan realized that he had a lot more information to look into. Since Father Beroni had been running the Outreach Program in a few locations, he decided to check them all out. Detective Shanahan brought with him his partner, Naomi Wright, whose investigative skills were extremely sharp and led to the soluteon of a number of cases they worked on. He suggested she go to the place where Negroni had been staying and check out anyone there who fit the description given by Mrs. Bronkowski. Naomi was familiar with many of the shelters, having helped many homeless people to find shelter and care. She was familiar with Father Beroni and the work he did to assist the homeless. As she entered the shelter, her penetrating eyes did a fast review looking for any Father Beroni look-a-likes. She had a conversation with the shelter director, Charles Walters, a slim, handsome man about 50 years old. He originally worked in the financial area, but like so many, found himself jobless. He discovered that by helping others he could help himself and in a conversation with his friend, Father Beroni, he discovered there was a need for someone with his talent, knowledge, and ability to run the shelter outreach program. As Charles and Naomi conversed, she filled him in on the additional information she and Dennis have discovered about someone else in the church at the time of the shooting. Charles told her that Father Beroni had not been around this shelter as much as previously, since he was working on establishing an additional shelter across town. As a result of this, he stopped in to all the Shelters when he could but not as often as he wanted to. Charles said that he remembered when the man who got shot came to this shelter, asking about Father Beroni. He told Charles that his name was William Negroni and he had some information that he wanted to talk to him about. I told him that Father was busy at the new location on West Side Avenue and the best time to catch him was between 1 pm and 2 pm over at Saint Albert's Church. Charles said he told Negroni that Father Beroni always kept the

Church poorly lit and heard confessions during those hours, because many people who had not been to church in years were hesitant to go to a big well-lit house of worship, but were more comfortable and willing to tell their sins in a quiet and dark environment. Charles said that Father Beroni discovered this one time when there was a power shortage, all the lights went out, and that day, he heard more confessions than he did in months. As result, from that time on, he let it be known that his dark and comfortable old Church was the place to come to relieve yourself of the old baggage of sin.

"You know, Naomi, come to think of it, the day Negroni asked about Father Beroni there was a guy who seemed very interested in our conversation. After Negroni left, the guy asked me where that church was, so I told him."

"Can you describe the guy for me? Does he stay at this shelter? Have you seen him since Negroni was shot?"

"The guy was not very big, probably no bigger than Father Beroni, and he looked like he had been out on the streets for a while. Come to think of it, I have not seen him since then."

"Charles, can you describe this guy for me?"

"He was not a very big guy. He had a scruffy beard and messy hair and looked like what you would expect a man who lived on the street to look like. We first invited him to consider staying at the shelter, but he did not like to be "indoors," as he put it. He did show up from time to time, especially when the weekly food truck showed up. He would take extra food with him when he left."

"You said he was interested in what Negroni was talking about. Did he say why?"

"No, he just wanted to know where the church was where Father Beroni was located. I told him where."

Naomi thanked Charles for giving her as much information as he had. "If he comes around again, please contact me or Dennis, right away. If he leaves before we get here, see if you can find out where he stays.

Thanks again."

Naomi left the shelter and met up

with Dennis.

"Hey Dennis, I have some new

information we need to look at."

"Before Negroni got shot, he asked

about Father Beroni. It seemed he

had information he wanted to talk

to Father about."

She then reviewed her conversation

with Charles Walters.

Dennis and Naomi reviewed the information they had. As they tried to assemble the facts now available, they began to see a pattern develop. They now had a strong, potential suspect surfacing. They needed to determine how this person fit into the picture of this crime. Having returned to the precinct they realized that they must reexamine all the evidence available. The gun revealed two sets of fingerprints.

The cop on the scene at the time of the incident just assumed the two sets represented the priest and the victim. The fact that the victim had no fingerprints was not known, until they tried to determine who he was, when he was brought to the hospital. As a result, the gun was simply tagged as evidence and put in the 'Evidence Locker.'

Detective Shanahan asked Detective Wright to have the gun reexamined by the lab for specific fingerprints, in an attempt to determine if it was

a legally licensed firearm or not.

As they went over the details,

Naomi's phone rang.

"Hello, this is Detective Naomi

Wright. Oh great, can you hold him

there, or at least find out where he

is staying. Dennis, that was Charles

Walters, the guy who asked about

Father Beroni just showed up at the

Shelter."

Naomi glanced over at Dennis, as he grabbed his jacket and said, "Let's get over there right now."

When they arrived, Charles told them that when he told the guy they were coming over, he ran out the door. Charles said he did get his name: Frank Johnson.

Dennis asked, "Do you know if he goes to any of the other Shelters?"

Charles said, "No, but we recently installed a front door CCTV and I believe we caught his picture

129

coming in. There have been some recent neighborhood break-ins, so we had to install this. We did not want it here on the inside, since it seemed too offensive for those who need this shelter."

He then pulled the video for Dennis and Naomi to see. They both thanked him and left to see if they could track him down.

Dennis asked Naomi to go back to the precinct and check if Frank Johnson showed up in any database.

Dennis decided to go see Father Don at the jail.

When Father Don saw Dennis, his first question was, "What are you doing here? I told you all I can tell you and the rest is under the seal of confession."

"Did you?" Dennis asked. "Ever hear of or speak to a Frank Johnson?"

"The name is not familiar to me, why do you ask?"

Before he could answer, his phone rang; it was the hospital. "That guy

in the coma just woke up and he
wants to talk to Father Beroni."

Dennis didn't answer Father's
question, and just said he had to go.
He left the room and then said into
his phone, "Don't tell him that
Father Beroni is in jail."

Dennis called Naomi, "I just got a
call from the hospital. Negroni is
out of the coma and wants to talk to
Father Beroni. Meet me at the
hospital."

Shanahan and Wright arrived at the hospital and went directly to the ICU to check on Negroni. The hospital staff were amazed that Negroni was awake and surprisingly alert.

"Mister Negroni, I am Detective Shanahan and this is Detective Wright. Do you remember being shot? Why did Father Beroni shoot you?"

Negroni said, "What do you mean? He didn't shoot me. Why would you say that?"

Shanahan recalled, "When we got the 911 call, we were told you were shot by the priest and the EMT's rushed you to the hospital to keep you alive."

Naomi said, "Please tell us what you remember about that day."

Negroni said, "I wanted to go to confession. I had information about this Father Beroni and I wanted to tell him that I knew who shot his father. He interrupted me to tell me that he knew who killed his father and for me not to worry about that. The next thing I knew, I felt this pain in my chest, then the noise of a shot, and then I woke up in this hospital."

Shanahan asked, "Did you know that someone was in the other side of the confessional?"

"I remember there was a guy from one of the other shelters. I did not know him but I felt like I had seen him before, when I was a kid in the old neighborhood."

Detective Wright asked, "Are you sure that Father Beroni did not shoot you?"

"He couldn't have, I felt the shot from the outside. I was a Marine and I know where bullets come from. There was no way that priest could shoot me from inside the confessional. Please have him come here. I want to talk to him."

Shanahan said, "It may take a while but I will bring him here myself."

They left and then Shanahan said to Wright, "Get them to release Father Beroni, since he did not do it.

Follow up that lead on Johnson and let's get him arrested for attempted murder."

About an hour later, Detective Wright called Shanahan and told him there was a holdup at a check cashing place and a homeless man was shot as the cops caught him in the act. They told her he was dead

at the scene. The homeless man was

Frank Johnson.

The Letter
Tom O'Rourke

"I just got a call that my wife is in this hospital. Can you tell me where she is?"

"Please calm down, sir. What is her name?"

"Sally Stein."

"Oh yes sir, she is in the ICU on the Second Floor. Unless you want to end up in the next bed, I suggest you calm down. Take that elevator (she points to the right) and when you get off at Two, follow the sign to the ICU."

When he steps into the elevator, his mind rushes back to the call he received from her earlier. *"I am going out to see one of my friends and I will be home later. By the way, I left an unsealed letter on the kitchen table, I'll explain it later."*

As he enters the ICU, the room is quiet, except for the sound of the oxygen and monitoring equipment. She appears to be asleep. The cast is on her left arm, so the intravenous drip is in the other. Her eyes are shaded purple and the slim poly tubing that feeds the oxygen to her nostrils is assisting her breathing. The medical team is concerned about internal bleeding. She may need a transfusion if it gets worse, or they may have to operate to find the exact source of the blood loss. Her condition is temporarily stable but demands constant observation.

Marvin hears the nurses talking about the police saying her car slid off the highway and down a short embankment. Had it gone a slight distance more it would have dropped more than one hundred feet into a rocky ravine. "She is lucky to be alive," is heard more than once as the medical team comes and goes, checking on her.

Sally has been a member of the county educational system for a number of years. She enjoys friends and acquaintances throughout the county, so Marvin was unsure who she was going to see. The police told Marvin that they got a call from someone in the neighborhood of the crash, who told them they heard loud noises and what sounded like a car accident. When the police arrived at the scene they saw no one else and no other vehicle. The skid marks appeared to reflect a quick stop and then an immediate turn across the road and then disappeared as the car went into the embankment. The police questioned him about his wife and were searching, by their questions, to determine his wife's mental state before the accident. They followed this line of interrogation, because they said that there were no signs of debris from a crash accident, only the skid marks and the car perched on the embankment.

"What did your wife tell you before she left? Who was she going to see? Were you and your wife having an argument before she left or were you fighting? Did either of you strike the other?"

"I come here to find my wife in an unconscious condition, bandaged, with an IV stuck in her arm and you are implying that I may have caused this? If I asked you that kind of question, you would probably pull your gun on me. What is your name?"

"I am Detective Franklin assigned by the county to investigate this accident. It is my responsibility to ask these kinds of questions so that we can determine how your wife ended up in that embankment."

Marvin was really angry and upset by this line of questioning, implying that their relationship was anything but a good one. Finally, Detective Franklin left the room as the nursing staff came in to check on the IV flow, as well as all the monitoring systems. This gave Marvin an opportunity to leave the room, go for a walk, and get a cup of coffee. His mind was racing through all the events of the last several hours. He thought about their last conversation and how upset Sally was.

"Marvin, I am having a tough time at this school. You know these middle school special education kids are pretty rough in the way they deal with authority figures. Some of these

are cruel and vicious hardcore students who should be watched very carefully because of their excessive physical strength and their uncontrollable behavior. A couple of them cursed and swore at me in an insulting way and the staff just brushed it aside."

Marvin remembers saying, *"I thought you really enjoyed working with these kids."*

She quickly came back with, *"Maybe it is time to consider retiring or at least work in a different environment."*

She talked about this at different times, so Marvin had not placed much stock in this kind of talk, figuring it is part of the job and will ease up after the school's spring break.

Had the situation gotten so bad that she ended up hurting herself? Marvin had provided her with a fine living, buying the house in the neighborhood she wanted, helping her select the finest furniture and the best automobile, and provided additional household help when it was needed. As far as he is concerned she has everything she needs. He has built up a fine and successful business. They have a typical American family, a boy and a girl, both of whom are now adults. Their son is married and has a son; their daughter is planning her marriage later in the year.

What more could she ask for?

What he cannot understand is how she actually feels. He is so busy, that he believes he is doing everything to give her what he believes she wants or needs. Her view of what they have together is different. He has a very controlling sense that only he would know what she wants and needs but she is looking for a different relationship with him.

Suddenly, Marvin hears Rex Harrison singing "Why Can't a Woman Be More Like a Man." The radio in the hospital lounge is playing music from Broadway plays and the *My Fair Lady* album is echoing through the speakers. Marvin finds himself laughing because this is exactly how he feels right now as he examines the relationship that he and Sally have. If only Sally saw things his way, everything would be fine. She looks at life in a more emotional and caring way and he is more routine and orderly. He is a preventive maintenance kind of guy and she waits for events to happen and then reacts to the situation. When they converse, she speaks from her emotional point of view.

"Marvin, I'm concerned about the kids. I don't think they realize how much I love them and want the best for them."

"Look Sally, we made sure they went to the best schools and have an opportunity to get the best of everything, even making sure they each have a good car and all they need."

"Now that they are on their own I don't get to see them as much as when they were living here at home. I miss them."

"Don't you understand that they both have careers now and are building their own future. I made sure they made the right contacts and were in the right place at the right time. Stop worrying, we did all we could for them."

"YOU did all that for them, but what did I do? I am just their mother. They don't think I did anything for them."

"What about us, Marvin? You were very attentive to me when we were *dating but now it's like I'm just part of the furniture. You don't seem to care about what is going on with me and what I need."*

"Of course I care for you. I make sure you have everything you need. I even make sure you are up to date on your meds so you don't have any more episodes."

"That's it Marvin, you just don't understand."

He doesn't hear the feeling she expresses but rather takes over the conversation and dictates what should be done. Their conversation ends with neither one of them understanding what the other actually said. In the hospital lounge, Marvin is reviewing all these conversations, in his head, and still cannot fathom why his wife may not be happy. Did she run this car off the road intentionally or is there a simpler explanation why the accident happened. He wants to determine her frame of mind.

His mental state is abruptly interrupted as he hears a "Code Blue" called over the hospital speakers. Assuming it is for Sally he turns quickly and runs back to the ICU unit. When he discovers the call was for another patient, he quickly realizes she could be gone in an instant. He is overwhelmed by the possibility of losing her.

 Then the doctor comes in.

"Mr. Stein, your wife's condition is more serious than it first appeared. In monitoring her blood condition, we discovered increased internal bleeding."

"Doctor, do whatever you need to do to take care of her."

The doctor expresses his understanding and tells him that they will do all they can.

"Her condition is very serious and you should be prepared for the unknown."

Marvin again pleads with the doctor to do whatever he has to do.

When they take Sally to the operating room, Marvin goes back to the lounge and plops down in an easy chair. Knowing that there is nothing he can do now, he hopes to take a nap while she is in the O. R. In seconds, he is off to dreamland. His dream takes him and Sally to their honeymoon island in Hawaii. The dream begins at the airport as they land. The marvelous greeting these newlyweds receive as they depart the plane makes them realize they have chosen a wonderful place to start their life together. The hotel room is covered with beautiful pink and yellow flowers and a table is set with champagne and a seafood sampling. Suddenly they are on a tour bus seeing all the sights on the island. The next moment they are in a helicopter flying over the islands of Hawaii and then they approach the volcano. Suddenly the helicopter has motor problems, it begins to rock and shake and then the motor dies. The helicopter falls rapidly into the volcano and then hits the bottom with a thud. Marvin feels a pull on his arm and is immediately awakened as a nurse asks him if he is okay. It seems the dream was so real for him that he was shouting about falling. Now, back to reality, he worries that this may indicate that Sally may not make it.

His cell phone rings and when he answers it, his son Stuart is on the phone asking about his mother.

"Dad, what happened, why is Mom in the hospital?'

Marvin reviews the news about Sally.

"How did that happen? Did anyone else get hurt? Is Mom Okay?"

"Your mother is the only one involved. There is no evidence of another car. The police are hinting at a suicide."

"Dad, has she been taking her meds? You know what happens when she doesn't."

"I was out all day so I don't know."

"Look I can get a flight out in the morning and be there before noon."

"Stuart, this trip is an important one for you and coming back tomorrow morning won't do anything to help.

She will be here for a spell, so finish the trip and come back when it is over. She'll be all right."

Marvin has always been a business first kind of guy and instilled in Stuart the same kind of thinking. Stuart says he will stay but insists that Marvin call him immediately if anything changes. They exchange good-byes and hang up.

Moments later, his daughter Carol calls, having just heard about her mother's accident. She is out in Washington on a major conference for her company but expresses serious concern for her mother.

"Dad I'll take the next plane out and be home tomorrow. "

"Carol, this conference is very important to you and your career, so stay and finish the conference. You cannot do anything to help your mother by coming here. The doctors and nurses are all doing everything they can."

"Dad, has Mom been taking her meds, or is this like that time she blacked out on the highway?"

"I was not at home today so I don't know. Just finish the conference and let me know when you are on your way home. Your mother will be okay."

She agrees but insists that he let her know immediately if anything changes. Marvin, in his attempt to stall reality, has convinced his children that maybe their mother is not in the most serious condition of her life.

Marvin now stares at the clock and wonders what is happening in the operating room. Have they found the problem? Are they able to correct it? Are they doing everything they can to bring her through? Questions, questions, questions, are there any answers?

His cell phone rings again, this time it is one of his major customers. He is surprised to get a call from a customer at this early hour of the day until he looks at his watch and discovers it is ten in the morning. He has been in the hospital since midnight. Marvin tells his customer that he will be out of touch for a while and his office will handle all business calls. He simply indicates that he has a serious family matter requiring his attention, but does not go into any detail. He then goes back to the Intensive Care Unit and discovers that Sally is not back from the operating room. His concern now intensifies. What if she doesn't make it? If she makes it what kind of therapy will she need? Will she need physical therapy, psychotherapy, occupational therapy, or all of these? Will she ever be able to return to a classroom again? Will she want to return, or does this end her career for good?

As he searches for these answers he reviews closely the time when she had a nervous breakdown (or at least that was what it seemed to be). The doctor, at the time, said it was due to excessive stress and he prescribed medication for her. The medicine appeared to have calmed her down and she resumed her normal activity. The doctor did require her to stay on the medication, which became routine. Now Marvin wonders if she's been taking her medication or has she decided she does not need it anymore. Worse, has she been taking more of it than prescribed?

Just then Detective Franklin returns with a zip top bag containing a number of prescription bottles.

"Mr. Stein, are these prescriptions your wife's? They were in the car."

"Yes, these are hers."

He does not say anything but he notices that they should have much more in each than they contain. Franklin is about to ask a question when they are interrupted by the doctor who has come to Marvin to talk to him about his wife.

"Mr. Stein, we were able to contain the bleeding but she is still in very serious condition. Do you know what medications your wife was taking? The bleeding seems to have been caused by both the accident and possibly excessive medication, not given by us in the hospital."

Marvin goes over the list with the doctor and indicates that to his knowledge, she has been faithful in taking the medications as prescribed and on time. The doctor suggests that in prescribed quantities there should be no problem, but an excessive amount of any or all can cause serious damage. The doctor then encourages Marvin to go home and rest since there is nothing more he can do and he needs his own rest. He assures Marvin that if there is any change he will notify him immediately.

Convinced by the doctor that Sally is resting and should be okay, he decides to return home. He wants to find that letter that Sally told him about and find out if that will enable him to figure out what happened.

It took him a short time, but he found the letter. When he opened it, it read simply: My Dear Marvin, There is so much I want to tell you, but I'm late for my appointment. I will finish this when I come home.

Just then the phone rang and it was the doctor, "Mister Stein, Your wife….." Marvin dropped the phone and fell to the floor.

Selfie World
Kathy Ravalli

While my husband and I were
strolling in Bay Ridge, we felt
raindrops fall on our heads. We
spotted a Starbucks and decided to
each order a tall cappuccino. As we
sat at a table and sipped our coffee,
we reminisced.

Chachi and Zoe decided they
should start spending time with
each other. He walked her home
after school and they studied
together. Zoe realized they had
several things in common the
minute they spent time together.
Zoe's friends were so happy to see

their friend finally with the boy she always liked. Zoe took many selfies of her and Chachi and taped them on the inside of her locker door.

After walking Zoe home from school for several days, Chachi finally asked Zoe out on a real date. They agreed to see a movie on a Saturday night, followed by having ice cream at Basin Robbins. Zoe had a super-duper time on her date with Chachi. Then he asked her to the prom!

Zoe was so excited, she had to call her friend and let her know that the boy she had a crush on all through high school just asked her to go to the prom. Zoe was so happy because she thought he never noticed her, and then voila, just weeks later, she had a prom date with Chachi! Zoe never had a boyfriend and she never felt pretty, but once the braces came off and she took her messy bun down, Chachi saw a different girl that he didn't want to let go of.

The first thing you need to know about me is that I wasn't always this beautiful blonde you know today. I know, it's shocking. The truth is, it wasn't that long ago that I was an awkward outcast with braces, with my hair up in a messy bun, wearing last year's clothes from Dee Dee and D11 that were two sizes too big.

'No, Zoe has always been perfect.' I can hear you disagreeing. Well, you're right, I have always been perfect on the inside, but that's a story for another time. Let me take you back so you can see that once upon a time, my struggle was deep and real.

I was fourteen years old and it was my first day at Brooklyn Performing Arts High School. The hallways were long and the students were tall. I came from a Catholic school and a sheltered

Catholic family. Until today, all I knew were the sweet familiar faces of the same twenty kids I grew up with. My parents decided I should go to a bigger school so I could meet more kids. I felt like a little fish in a large pond. I stood out like a sore thumb and yes, I did have all the kids looking and staring at me as well.

On the first day of high school, I woke up late and failed to get my outfit ready the way I had envisioned. The frilly white blouse, black pants, and knee-high boots that Taylor Swift pulled off so effortlessly had me looking less like a pop star. Don't ask me how I survived the first day after being made fun of.

At home, my parents asked me the awful question every kid dreads hearing. The question that sounded like nails on a chalkboard. "How was your day?" "Fine," I lied. Then I changed my mind and told them the truth. "Actually it was terrible because the school was ginormous and everyone thought they were so cool." I said. My mom said, "Are you sure, because none of them are as cool as you." I replied, "Thanks mom, I'll make sure to tell the kids at school that my mom thinks I'm super cool."

      The next morning when I got to school, I went to my locker and there happened to be a girl standing right next to my locker eating a York Peppermint Patty. She had red hair and freckles and I thought to myself, 'Oh my gosh, it's Peppermint Patty from Charlie Brown!' We started up a conversation and we decided that we should be friends because she was new at the school, as well. Now that I finally had a friend, I no longer had to rely on selfies and social media as my only source of meeting new friends. Peppermint Patty was the type of girl that I could find myself calling or hanging out with. I knew she would be a friend - a friend who would never judge me.

Now that you know a little bit of my history, let's go back to reality. I met this wonderful guy named Chachi and he asked me to prom which was weeks away. My mom bought me this beautiful prom gown from David's Bridal and Chachi told me he had the most beautiful corsage picked out, and that he already ordered it for me. As the days wound down, I became more and more excited. I planned on wearing my hair in an up-do with a whole bunch of curls. I knew this would be a day that would last a lifetime. I also knew we would be taking a lot of pictures, so it was very important that I looked my best.

"The sun is back out," Chachi declared. "We can get back to our walk now. Although I do love reminiscing about our past AND looking at all the pictures."

Awaiting New Jerusalem
Elizabeth H. Theofan

<u>Abigail</u>

Last Sunday, just like every
other Sunday, I was attending our
Calvinist Reform Protestant church
in the center of town. It was a plain
box without even a steeple, and it
wasn't even the biggest building in
Jerusalem, New Mexico in 1872. It
was hot. The pews smelled like
they were about to ignite. All
around, the plain glass windows
were opened, letting in the grit of
the desert like an hourglass. The
longer we stayed the more sand
was scattered on the broad planked

floor. I wished for stained glass windows like the Catholic church. At least that would have cast some shade. But for us, the depictions were considered idol worship.

Our grey-haired pastor was the only man I knew that did not have a ruddy face and he was the only man I knew who wore glasses all of the time. Listening to him was my only opportunity to hear the full measure of a man's voice with its cadence and pitch. He was the only man I ever heard speak more than a few sentences at a time. His was the voice that was the narrator in my dreams.

Our pastor started reading the Gospel lesson: *And it came to pass, when the time was come that Jesus should be received up, steadfastly set his face upon Jerusalem.*[1]

That was the last thing I heard him say because my mind was turned to the time before I could remember. I started thinking about my father who steadfastly set his face upon this Jerusalem in 1855. That is where we lived ever since. He decided to move out west after the Gold Rush, but before the Civil War and more importantly

---

[1] Luke 9:51 KJV

before the collapse of the whaling industry. My mother and father moved from Salem, Massachusetts right before I was born. *And Melchizedek King of Salem brought forth bread and wine and he was the priest of the most high God.*[2] My mother frequently reminded me that the Jerusalem in the Bible was first named Salem.

I was twelve years old when my mother died. That has to be the worst possible age. I was old enough to appreciate what a wise and beautiful lady she was but I was too young to benefit from the

---

[2] Genesis 14:18 KJV

advice that she had yet to tell me. Now I am seventeen years old. There are so many questions I could have asked her. There are so many ways that I am on my own.

My mother died before she could have known that my father made a good financial decision to leave Salem. Being in the whaling business, my father realized that he was taking bigger and bigger risks. Because of over-harvesting, whales were harder to find. Ships had to be sent our further into the treacherous north Atlantic Ocean in order to find whales to kill and to process into precious lamp oil.

Twelve years later whale oil was being replaced rapidly by cheaper and cleaner petroleum oil. If he would have stayed, my father would have been ruined financially.

I wonder if that information would have made any difference to my mother. She died of a broken heart because she was homesick for Salem. In his mind, my father thought he did everything he could to please her. He even built our house as an exact replica of the home where she lived with her parents before they were married. There was even a "widow's walk" on top. In Salem that was used to spot the ships returning from sea. In addition, our house had gables, turrets and a wrap-around-porch. The exterior had slate blue shingles accented with rich red and gold. Unfortunately, in just a few years the desert sun scoured almost all of the color away.

I remember the last day that I saw my mother sitting on the porch. I had just walked out of the front door, when I silently glided up almost to where she was sitting. As she stared ahead she looked as if she was looking for something that wasn't there. From her porch in Salem she would have been looking directly at the sea. As I looked at her face I saw a tear falling from her eye. I didn't even think she knew that I was there. All of a sudden she turned to me, and, in a voice that was eerie and full of finality, she said:

"Abigail, you look like me and your eyes are the blue-grey color of the sea. Yet you are more your father. Yes, you like the Bible and intellectual pursuits like I do, but you are not a person who is dependent on other people. You are a person of pure action, able to thrive on your own. You will be able to survive this desolate place."

My mother got up, walked in the front door and went directly into her study which was full of nautical brass implements, scrimshaw art pieces, dolls in a sailor outfits and oil paintings of ships at sea. While inside, she could make believe that she was still in Salem, in a house with the sea outside its door, the sea with its winds, its roaring sounds and its fullness of life sporting and playing in all its mystery. She could try to forget the monotone wilderness.

Within a week, my beautiful mother was dead. She didn't wake up one morning. I was not surprised – sad - but not surprised. At least she had said her last words to me while on the porch. My father still has a hard time looking at me. Although I would like to, I never wear any of her beautiful dresses.

One of my mother's favorite accounts in the Bible was Jesus' Temptation in the wilderness which took place before starting his ministry. *After Jesus' baptism "immediately the spirit driveth him into the wilderness forty days, tempted of Satan; and was with the wild beasts; and the angels ministered unto him."*[3] My mother

_____

[3] Mark 1:12-13 KJV

envied Jesus because he was able to leave the wilderness. In order to leave, even he needed help. He needed the angles to minister to him.

Sometimes I wonder, even now, if the wilderness, any wilderness but especially our New Mexican wilderness, is the home of the devil. After all that's where Jesus was driven to meet up with him. We know that Satan walks around: *And the Lord said unto Satan, Whence comest thou? Then Satan answered the Lord, and said, From going to and fro in the earth,*

and from walking up and down in it.
⁴

    I hope that I am not being disrespectful to God. But, at least to me, the wilderness seems to be outside of his creative order. *So God created man in his own image in the image of God created he him; male and female created he him. And God blessed them, and God said unto them, Be fruitful and multiply, and replenish the earth, and subdue it; and have dominion over the fish of the sea, and over the fowl of the air, and over every living thing that*

---

[4] Job 1:7 KJV

moveth upon the earth.[5]   But there is no subduing the wild animals of the wilderness where they do the devil's bidding.

My mother must have felt as Adam and Eve did when they were cast out of Paradise. She so longed for her past life-filled connections of family, friends, church gatherings, concerts and lectures. Her pain and loneliness was so acute that she talked for hours about Salem. She spoke in such detail about everyone she knew, that after a while, not only could I repeat all of her stories, but I felt

<hr>

[5] Genesis 1:27-28 KJV

like I had actually known everyone she ever met. After God expelled Adam and Eve from Paradise he *placed at the east of the garden of Eden Cherubims, and a flaming sword which turned everyway.*[6] When my mother was "expelled" from her paradise, there was most of a vast continent west of Salem that was preventing her from ever returning.

So many times my mother said that there was no collective culture, wisdom or knowledge in or near Jerusalem, New Mexico. She thought that there had to be some

---

[6] Genesis 3:24 KJV

concentration of people in a place for these qualities to prosper. She liked to talk about Wisdom, the great feminine figure in the Bible who could have been a comfort in the wilderness but she was not there. Wisdom, in the Book of Proverbs, calls out in order to teach people who already fear the Lord how they ought to live. *Doth not wisdom cry? and understanding put forth her voice? She standeth in the top of high places, by the way in the places of the paths. She crieth at the gates, at the entry of the city, at the coming in at the doors.*[7] She visits

_____

[7] Proverbs 8:1-3 KJV

where people live, work, interact together. In Jerusalem I've tried to picture Wisdom walking about while crying out, but I just couldn't. There was too much desert dust sifting through the streets. Furthermore, even if she would enter, she would leave immediately, when seeing that greatest building was not the church, but the bank. Like every other building, it was bleached by the destroying sun.

Recently, I overheard my father, Hezekiah, talking about me to the owner of the cattle ranch that was next to ours. I wonder if my father knew who his namesake was in the Bible? *He trusted in the Lord God of Israel; so that after him was none like him among all the kings of Judah, nor any that were before him.*[8] My father was respected by the men of Jerusalem and was considered to be its greatest leader. He served on every important board and civic organization. But he had no son to succeed him.

When I heard their voices, I was in, what was now, my study. I was reading the Bible and taking notes to prepare the Sunday school lesson. I did this each week. But unlike my mother who secluded

_____

[8] 2 Kings 18:5 KJV

herself when she sat there, I wanted to know everything that was going on around me, so I always kept the door partially opened. I listened to my father and his friend planning on matching their children up. Well, that was about the last thing on my mind. I really didn't think of marriage as an accomplishment and I was not interested.

My greatest accomplishment would be to fulfill Jesus Christ's Great Commission to bring people to him. He commanded all of us to do this when he spoke to his Disciples just before he ascended into heaven. *And Jesus came and spake unto them, saying, All power is given unto me in heaven and in earth. Go ye therefore, and teach all nations, baptizing them in the name of the Father, and of the Son, and of the Holy Ghost: Teaching them to observe all things whatsoever. I have commanded you and lo, I am with you always even unto the end of the world. Amen.[9]*

How could I bring anyone to Jesus? Everyone I know socially attends our church. The Mexican women who work in our home are devout Catholics. They have fun in their church with its pageantry,

---

[9] Matthew 28:19-20 KJV

festivals and they even get to pray to a woman – the Virgin Mary. I am not permitted to speak to any of the men who are employed on my father's vast cattle ranch so I can't reach out to them.

My greatest fulfillment was in teaching Sunday School. Since their parents are believers, their children have already been told about Jesus. But, I am (at least I hope I am) bringing them even closer to Jesus. I love children. They are so beautiful and so eager to learn. The girls are smarter, sometimes a little too smart, and very independent, but they are respectful. The boys are so cute. They seem to be a little confused at times and they definitely want my help. That makes me love the boys a little more. Their eyes still have color; their lips are still full. They can still ask for help. They still have an imagination. They still care about people's feelings.

But what happens when they grow up? With the possible exception of our pastor, all of the grown men that I know, including my father, are interested only in tangible things; money, cattle, the bank, governing, ruling and power. Where is the little boy in them?

Where is the wonder? Where is the concern for other people's feelings, even those closest to them? Where are the deep blue eyes and the red rounded lips?   The grown men of Jerusalem all have pale blue eyes, almost as clear as water, like there is no reflection back into them from anything that is beautiful. They all have a thin pale pink line where there once were lips, like they atrophied, because they stopped smiling so long ago.

I listened a little more to the conversation about a possible suitor for me. I had never so much as held hands with a man. I

certainly had never been kissed. I
never had a gentleman caller. I got
up from my desk so I could hear
more of what was being said. I had
a hard time believing that my father
could talk for this long, especially
about me. He must really want an
heir very badly.

"Your daughter is a beautiful
young lady, very accomplished.
Even my grandsons who are holy
terrors like going to Sunday School.
I think that she would be a good
bride for my youngest son,
Michael."

"I remember Michael, good
looking boy, smart. How old is he?"

"He's twenty-years-old, will be graduating from Harvard next year. After that he plans to apprentice to become an attorney with old John Jay Nichols in Jerusalem."

"Sounds perfect for my Abigail. She needs to be with an accomplished scholar."

"I agree. She would be a great asset to Michael, a help in many ways."

It all sounded interesting but I was apprehensive. Harvard was at least near Salem, very civilized. Obviously he liked to read. I liked his name, thinking of the Archangel Michael. *And there was war in heaven: Michael and his angels fought against the dragon; and the dragon fought and his angels, And prevailed not; neither was their place found any more in heaven.*[10] But, this Michael is probably like all of the rest of the men I know. I was not convinced that any man retained any of the precious emotional qualities of my Sunday School boys. After all, I watched my own father not care at all about my mother's pain even though he was

---

[10] Revelation 12:7-8 KJV

considered by everyone to be a good man.

Then, I decided to go out to the porch to sit for a while before the sun set. My mother told me about the glorious sunrises and sunsets in Salem. They were slow, gradually displaying the whole spectrum of yellows, oranges and reds that bounced off clouds against the backdrop of the cool blue shades of the sky and sea. Here in Jerusalem the sun conducts business like everyone and everything else. It comes up suddenly, without any help from the clouds, a round red ball rising above a straight line and down again the same way. It was either daytime – light or it was nighttime – dark. Although my mother told me about it, I still have a hard time picturing the moon reflecting a trail along the sea at dusk. Maybe someday I will see it.

Lines, lines and more lines, horizontal, vertical, not even a diagonal. There were fence posts, straight roads, even the buildings had flat roofs. By looking at the horizon you would think that the world was flat. The only exception was our home, but that was because of my mother. If it weren't for her even it would be a rectangle.

Luke

My leg hurts. It throbs and burns but not worse than my head. The horse that just threw me was not my horse but belonged to my older brother Mark. Mark is dead. My horse is dead. My oldest brother Matthew is dead. I couldn't control this horse with my broken leg, so he threw me. The horse probably thought that since my brothers were shot to death that I should be dead too. Most people would laugh at this but I've always known how horses think. I'd rather talk with them than with people. To them, I usually don't know what to say.

Now I sit alone in the desert, unable to stand up. If I'm still here tonight, the wild animals will kill me, rip me apart and the devil will laugh. I know he's here in the desert getting closer. My only hope is that the posse catches me soon. At least for a while, I'll enjoy some time resting on a clean cot in jail. Until I am hanged maybe I'll eat the same food that the Marshall's wife cooks for him.

I have no protection. My gun dropped before I rode away. My

two brothers and I were part of the Dixie Disciples gang. We tried to rob the Sherman Cooper Bank in Jerusalem. No one got any money, not even coins to cover the eyes of the dead.

A wise old Mexican man told me that when you're about to die all of your life comes together in your mind and you understand what you deserve. I know that I deserve to go to hell. One way or another, devil is about to take me.

Unfortunately, I have so many, add another many, regrets. To say that circumstances are an excuse is wrong. My mother read the Bible every day. Sometimes she told me things about what it said. She told me, because my older brothers wouldn't even listen. I listened because I really felt for her and I was glad that the Bible gave her happiness and peace. There was one verse that she made me memorize. I still remember it.

There hath no temptation taken you but such as is common to man: but God is faithful, who will not suffer you to be tempted above that ye are able; but will with the temptation also make a way to escape, that ye may be able to bear it.[11]

---

[11] 1 Corinthians 10:13 KJV

Well, I failed to escape temptation. My descent into sin started at age fourteen. That's when I followed my brothers out of Missouri. That was four years ago. My brothers were several years older and this was the first time that they included me in anything. Two years before, my mother died while giving birth to our baby brother John. He died a few hours later. By then our farm was in ruins, caused by Yankee soldiers right before the end of the Civil War. Like we had anything to do with the war. We owned no slaves; were much too poor. My father, mother, brothers and I worked like slaves, but gladly, because our effort yielded a livelihood for ourselves. I can't imagine working even harder than we did especially for a master who didn't even consider people he owned to be human beings. Even if we had the money, we would have never bought slaves. We even hid and fed escaped slaves in our root cellar when they needed shelter while they were on their way north to freedom. But none of that mattered. Our farm was destroyed.

That destruction started the smell, the smell of sin and death.

Before that all around us were the heavenly smells. Outside, the smell of growing crops.   Inside, the smell of new wood and delicious cooking. After the destruction there was the smell of dirty mud outside and although we tried to repair our home, the acrid smell from the flames never went away. It was the smell of brimstone.

My mother died in 1866. She didn't have enough to eat to have the strength to carry a baby. Even the few cows and pigs that we had left had young that was stillborn or lived for only a few hours like poor baby John. The issue blood of the animals was not sweet smelling like a healthy birth but the coppery smell of the blood of death. My father expired two years later in 1868, drank himself to death. He stank worse and worse as alcohol rotted him from the inside until he was just a heap of twisted flesh. Then mercifully, he was gone.

All that was left were the three of us. I had nowhere to go but with Matthew and Mark. They were grown men while I was just fourteen when we left the farm. It was no longer ours, repossessed by the bank.

Matthew and Mark always, or so it seemed, knew what to do and where to go. I stopped asking questions because they would laugh at me. I wanted a direction, a reason why I was even alive. They were comfortable with hate and revenge.

For two years we traveled back and forth between Texas and Louisiana. From what I saw, you would think that slavery never ended. The Negroes worked so hard that I could smell their salty sweat and tears. And I could smell something else, the smell of decay everywhere that the Yankees destroyed.

At first my brothers lived by low level crime, shoplifting, cattle rustling and stealing crops. They never involved me until New Mexico when they became more violent. Matthew and Mark figured that I was ready to join them at sixteen. By then I looked like a man, tall and filled out. I really didn't want to do anything illegal but by then Matthew and Mark got so mean that I was more afraid of them than of the law or, God forgive me, than even Jesus.

Today I watched four men die, two bank guards and my two brothers. The smell of strangers' blood mixed with the smell of my family blood made me sick. When my horse, Jubilee, was shot he fell and rolled over and broke my leg. I then grabbed Mark's horse, Stonewall, and had to force him to leave his dead owner. I knew that I was doomed. I should feel sad. I should be in mourning. But for so long I knew that this would happen. It's almost a relief that it is all over.

Now I sit in agony ready for death thinking about my biggest regret that I never kissed a good woman. Before our troubles I saw the way my father admired my mother in pure respect and love. That's what I wanted. I'm eighteen, I would have probably been engaged by now to a good woman if things had stayed the same.

Oh, I'm no virgin. My brothers took me to a sporting house in New Orleans two years ago. The parlor had furniture that felt like they were full of pillows when you sat down on them. I had never seen chairs and couches in such rich reds and purples. There were more fringes on the oil lamps than on an Indian's coat. There was a Creole band playing the best music I ever heard. My brothers went upstairs one at a time. I was dizzy from what I thought were flowers, but there didn't seem like there were enough of them for that much of a smell. It was like a funeral parlor. Finally, I figured out that the prostitutes were soaked in perfume. The smells were fighting each other, each creating their own layer in the hot humid air. Mark could see that I was getting sick so he gave me a drink, my first ever. It smelled like the medicine that we used to give the cows and tasted so bad I wanted to spit it out. Finally, it was my turn. I was seriously thinking about how to run out back when she appeared, broad enough to block the light of God and man. There it was, the shadow of sin and death. I could hear my mother's voice. All of a sudden I remember how she warned me about prostitutes by quoting the Bible. All I could remember was: *Her feet go down to death, her steps take hold in hell.*[12] I followed her steps anyway.

The first thing I noticed in her room was the wallpaper. It was the same wallpaper that hung in our parlor at home. I vaguely listened

---

[12] Proverbs 5:5 KJV

while looking around as she introduced herself as Rose. As inexperienced as I was, I knew that was not her real name. I was both fearful and grateful that she directed the encounter. I knew what animals on the farm did but I had no idea how humans went about it.

"Look at me," Rose said and I finally did. She had eyes that could have been made out of the marbles that I used to play with, both surrounded by deep wrinkles. There was stuff all over her face that looked like gunpowder. When she sneered I noticed some rotten teeth. The devil was speaking through them. She told me to strip. I almost welcomed that part because I was sweating as bad as I did when I used to milk our cows during July and August. She then examined me like my father did when buying a bull to make sure that it wasn't diseased. Rose then ordered me to get into her bed. The scented candles on either side of it couldn't hide the smell of sweat of all of the men who lay there that night. She didn't take anything off. Apparently she wore no underwear because she straddled me and laughed. Three minutes later it was over.

"Come back soon, you're a cutie for sure." I heard her say and then laugh. I put my clothes back on as quickly as I could. That's all it was, not even a kiss. I was smart enough to hide in a niche in the hallway before going downstairs to my brothers waiting to hear all about it. Of course I said it was great. It was pathetic.

So here I was, never knowing love from a good woman, never been kissed, living four years in sin, with my mother, father, and brothers dead, wanting to die but not looking forward to going to hell, when she arrived. At first I thought she was a mirage.

Abigail

A horse, someone falling. I saw it from the porch while wishing to see something other than dust before the end of the day. I ran over and found him. It was like he was waiting there for me. He was a young man with golden hair that matched the stubble on his cheeks and chin. But what was even more noticeable were his eyes. They were as blue as the sky at noon, too blue to belong to the palette of the landscape. He had to be from somewhere in the east. Although his mouth was askew I could see that he had real lips. He was handsome but that's not the only thing that made him different.

Somehow I was not startled to find him there. Somehow I was not afraid. He looked like he was in pain and he looked like he was lost, really lost. I could tell by the way he was sitting that his leg was broken. I felt like if I was going to help him at all, I would have to do it right away. He was the only grown man that I had ever met who needed, and somehow I just knew, wanted my help. I told him that I

would be right back to bring him a
sandwich and some water.

Luke

She was real. The air around her
was like my mother's flower and
vegetable garden. Somehow I knew
that she would come back. I never
thought I would see that look again.
She looked at me like my mother
did – with care in her eyes. Not
even in my dreams did I think that I
would be near a woman like her.
She was beautiful on the outside
and a light seemed to emanate
through her. She was like a woman
in the Bible.

I wanted her to talk with me. Somehow I wasn't afraid. I knew she would help me.

There she was, coming back like she promised.

Abigail and Luke

"My name is Abigail."

"Mine is Luke."

"Like the Apostle."

"I wish, but I'm not."

"Where are you from?"

"Originally from Missouri, but now from nowhere."

"This is nowhere."

"Please, you have to tell them where I am, so they can come get me. I can't walk and the devil will make sure that the animals rip me apart if I stay."

"Are you from the bank robbery?"

"Yes, but I didn't kill anyone, but I will be hanged because I was there. Two bank guards and both of my brothers were killed."

"Are you afraid?"

"Not to die, but I am afraid of going to hell."

"That's not true if you believe in Jesus. Do you?"

"I did when my mother was alive. In a way maybe I still do, but now I am unworthy to believe in him."

"That's not true! No one is unworthy to believe in Jesus. Would you like to come back to him?"

"It's not too late?"

"It is never too late."

"There's hope?"

"There's more than hope, there's certainty."

"What's heaven like?"

"Well it's nothing like here in this wilderness where we are all tested."

"And we can leave?"

"Yes, with the help of the angels, just like they helped Jesus. We can follow Jesus to the City of God."

"What is the City of God? Please tell me. I really want to know."

"It's the New Jerusalem. Not the Jerusalem where we are today. In the Book of Revelation John described it to us as: *And I saw a new heaven and a new earth, the holy city, New Jerusalem, coming down from God out of heaven. And God shall wipe away all tears from their eyes; and there shall be no more death, neither sorrow, nor crying, neither shall there be any more pain; for the former things are passed away."*[13]

"Do you believe that Jesus Christ is your Lord and Savior?"

"I have been blessed to believe that all my life."

"I can see you do."

---

[13] Revelation 21:1,4 KJV

The wind then blew hard, like a whirlwind, like the Holy Spirit on the day of Pentecost. Suddenly, Luke was filled. Luke was at peace when he said:

"I accept Jesus Christ as my Lord and Savior."

"I'm so happy Luke. Thank you!"

Abigail, you must go back home. I don't want you to be associated with me. Just tell them you saw someone fall in a distance. I'm ready for them. But there is only one thing I ask before you go."

"What is it Luke?"

"Can you kiss me?"

There it was – the first kiss. They were both surprised that lips could be so soft and warm. Although it lasted for only a short time, it changed both of them. To Luke it was the *alpha and omega,*[14] the first and the last. For a very brief moment he was on the farm, the farm that he should have had but would never own with the bride that would never be his. For Abigail it was the key to her future. All of the sudden with her eyes closed she could see *a pure river of life, clear as*

---

[14] Revelation 1:8 KJV

crystal[15] flowing right through the desert. It was possible that life could be found in this wilderness. A man could have all of the attributes that she wanted. He could be brave in facing death and at the same time be sensitive enough to care about her thoughts and strong enough to ask for her help. Neither of them saw the other's tears as Abigail walked away.

It was Wednesday. He knew he would be hanged on Friday. All lawful hangings in the territory were done on Fridays. It

---

[15] Revelation 22:1 KJV

was the same day of the week that Jesus was crucified.

Jerusalem Evening Dispatch

June 21, 1872

<u>Murderous Thief Hanged</u>

Today at high noon, eighteen-year-old Luke Stevens of the Dixie Disciples gang, was hanged for attempted robbery and for the murder of the two Sherman Cooper Bank guards. At least one hundred men watched while

Stevens refused a hood. His broken right leg was braced so that he could stand on the gallows platform.

The heat of the day and the pain from his leg must have affected him because in his delirium the last words he said were: "Good-bye everyone. I know I am going to heaven because I was helped by an angel."

Luke Stevens was survived by no one.

The Day I Grew Up
Elizabeth H. Theofan

Every Saturday afternoon my best friend Karen and I went somewhere together just to have fun. We had been best friends since we met in junior high school in Park Slope, Brooklyn. Very quickly we found out that we had a lot in common since we both grew-up in strict homes and we both had grandparents who were born on "the other side." Neither one of us had ever been to "the other side" but we knew we hated it and never wanted to go. In fact, we were the second generation who hated it.

None of our parents had ever wanted to go across the Atlantic Ocean either.

It was a Saturday, a lot like any other Saturday. We were seniors at John Jay High School. It was April and we were both excited about going to college in the fall. I had been accepted to Cooper Union to major in Civil Engineering and Karen had been accepted to Brooklyn College to major in Biology and Pre-Med. It was 1968, a time of great changes in society, but our homes were holding steady. In fact, the scene was schizoid. We were encouraged to do well in school and to strive for professional careers, but even though we were seventeen years old, we were not allowed to date. In fact, neither of us were allowed to wear make-up. If I were to tell that to any seventeen-year-old girl today she would think that I was delusional. Besides, we wouldn't have known what to do on a date anyway. Karen was wary about talking to boys. She came from a family of three girls with a confident mother and a lunatic father. He hollered so much that everyone ignored him. Ergo, Karen thought that all males were put on this earth to be ignored.

I didn't have any sisters, just a brother who was two years younger. He was very funny and we joked around constantly, but always out of earshot of our mother who found it annoying. My father, who worked long hours, joked with my brother and me, whenever he was home, about everything from politics to sports. He especially liked goofing on members of the extended family. So unlike Karen, I thought that all males were put on this earth to amuse me.

Karen and I talked about guys just as much as the girls who had boyfriends. But unlike them we concentrated our energies on the rich and famous. I liked Jack Lord on Hawaii 5-0 while she liked William Schatner on Star Trek. As big baseball fans we had our favorites there too. I liked Sandy Koufax while Karen liked Don Drysdale. The trend was that I liked the dark haired guys while she liked guys with lighter features. It was great!   The world of handsome men was equally divided and we weren't competing against each other.

It's funny in a way, that we made fun of our grandmothers who barely spoke English while we were being raised with the same social ground rules. You have to live at home until you get married and nothing goes on until the honeymoon. Some of the other girls who were getting ready to go away to college felt sorry for us. Little did they know that neither one of us wanted to go away.

Not being allowed to date had plenty of advantages. Karen and I didn't have to be thin. We could enjoy our food as long as we weren't fat enough to be made fun of. Besides, our families associated fashionable thinness with being on death's door. There was no reason to worry them.

Without the high drama of romance we had clear heads for our studies. Since that came easy to both of us anyway we each had plenty of time for extracurricular reading on virtually every subject. Our mothers taught us all of the domestic arts. Karen specialized in knitting while I excelled in intricate embroidery. Both of us helped our mothers with household chores and we were already good cooks. What catches we were – but not yet!

We were loved by our parents and extended families. Both of us were stars because of our academic achievements and for following all of the house rules gladly. I always felt sorry for the girls who had no rules. The rules gave us our place in life. All of this lead to us being secure, confident, and slightly chubby, not overly concerned with fashion, and relaxed enough to be intuitive, funny and carefree. Our brand of carefree wasn't the sexy image of a model with hair flowing in the wind. Our carefree was goofing on everything like kids but with an impressive knowledge base. The whole thing must have seemed strange to – well just about everyone.

Karen and I met every Saturday at 1:00 p.m. That's after we completed our household chores. Depending on the season or the weather we would enjoy one of the following: a movie, shopping, Brooklyn Botanical Gardens, a museum or just take a very long walk to check out a different neighborhood in Brooklyn or Manhattan. At the end of each activity we would always go out to eat. A great deal of out Saturday afternoon conversation would revolve around what to eat and where. The only criteria were that the restaurant be near home and inexpensive. We were always home by 6:00 p.m. We didn't have a curfew because we didn't need one.

That Saturday, I was worried that I would be late in meeting Karen. Just at the last minute my mother asked me to iron an elaborately embroidered doily. I could tell by the design that it was from Greece.

"Is this another one from grandma?" I asked my mother.

"Yes, this one was made by a girl who lives in grandma's home village. She is even younger than you are."

"Does this go into the closet like the others?"

"Yes, it does."

"Mother, you're running out of room on the doily shelves."

"That's all right; I just can't get rid of any of them. Each of the women and girls who worked on the doilies spent many days straining their eyes to do such fine work."

With that I ran and put the doily in the closet with all of the others. Then I dashed out of the door with thoughts of the Brooklyn Botanic Gardens.

In twenty minutes Karen and I got there after walking for one and a half miles. We had been to the gardens so many times over the years that we could anticipate what plant would bloom and where. Both of us were so well read in botany that we were experts. Any change, any new plant, any new bench or even any new rock was noticed by either one or both of us immediately.

We walked very fast in our practically orthopedic shoes and spoke really loudly and jumped up and down and giggled like kids when we saw anything particularly beautiful. That day even before we got down the steps on the big hill I smelled it.

"The lilac! It's blooming!"

"Yeah, the lilac!" Karen answered.

We ran down the hill. That must have looked "graceful." I saw some people look at us with annoyance. Who cares? We truly enjoyed the lilac and everything else in the gardens.

One of our favorite things to do was to follow the stream and to walk across each of its little bridges. We did it twice that day to the small pond at the end of the stream and back towards the main entrance. This way we checked out the daffodils, tulips and other blooming spring flowers twice.

On our way back from the pond a really good looking guy was standing under the biggest weeping willow tree in the whole garden. As usual, I spotted him first.

"Hey Karen, good looking guy alert!"

"Where, where?"

"Under the tree, and he's one of yours – a blond."

"Oh wow! He is good looking and he's even wearing a Brooklyn College jacket."

"Do you want to Bunker Hill it?"

"You mean don't leave until we see the color of his eyes?"

"Yeah!"

We both laughed.

As we got closer we could see that he had incredible sky-blue eyes. But unfortunately for our imaginations we could also see that he had a girlfriend.

"Sorry Karen, he's taken."

"Yeah, but look at her. Her legs are so skinny that it's a miracle that she can walk."

"And what's with her dyed brassy blond hair? What's wrong

with having dark hair like us? At least she could get her black roots done."

"And if she used one more puff of hairspray the whole thing would be weighted down enough to fall off of her head."

"But you have to admit Karen that she has perfect skin. There's not a zit on it and I swear it looks like she doesn't even have pores."

Yeah, her skin looks good for now. Remember what our mothers' say."

In unison we repeated their adage: "Pimples now means no wrinkles later." It's incredible that our mothers actually had us convinced that having the occasional pimple was far better than having flawless skin.

"The guy's young. He doesn't know any better. Don't worry, in about ten years from now you'll be allowed to date. Then he'll be mature enough and ready for you, Karen."

We both laughed.

Soon our thoughts turned to matters that were of more immediate importance to us. As we were walking out of the gate onto Eastern Parkway I asked:

"O.K., where are we eating?"

"So do you want to try a new place?" answered Karen with a question.

"Sure, what kind and where?"

"There's a new Greek restaurant on Seventh Avenue."

"Oh yeah, I saw it. Do you know anything about it?"

"No, how should I know? I thought that by now that you would know all about it. After all you're the one who's Greek."

"So do you know every Italian restaurant?"

We laughed.

"O.K., yeah, why not. I'll go. Maybe they'll have eggplant spread," I said.

"Mmm! I hope that the portions are big enough.

"Yeah, I hope so. Remember the last place we went we got hardly anything to eat."

Like we would ever starve. Our concept of an individual portion was enough to feed a family of four. Lately we were starting to wonder if the rest of America ate like our families did.

We walked for over two miles. We may have been chubby, but with our constant walking, gym every day at school, and the vigorous housework, we were strong and fit. When we got to the restaurant we could see that it wasn't fancy. We checked out the menu posted on the door. It was well within our price range. So we went right in. The place was empty. We gave each other looks that asked "Why?"

"Hello girls, sit, sit, anywhere you like. Welcome, you'll like it." That's how the old Greek woman greeted us in her broken English. She could have been my grandmother's twin. That put me on red alert. Even if the food wasn't great I was glad to be there. There was plenty of material for my jokes and sarcastic remarks.

The day we sat down in this little Greek restaurant, America was still striving to be a melting pot, not the mosaic that politicians and academic types talked about decades later when things weren't melting fast enough. Well Karen and I were just about melted. She didn't speak Italian and I didn't speak Greek. My mother's parents did everything they could to be American and even raised their children as Protestants. But my father's mother may still have been living in Greece. She's the one I always goofed on and her twin was now hovering over us. Karen had the same family dynamic even though they all remained Roman Catholic. Her father's mother was the real Italian. We rarely talked about the Americanized grandparents; no fun.

Twin-gramma handed us the menus. I was expecting a more extensive food list than what was posted on the door, but all of the essentials were there except for the eggplant spread. From where I was sitting I faced the back of the restaurant. From my vantage point I could look into the kitchen. I saw a short little man about 45-years-old who must have been the cook. He looked pathetic.

As always, Karen and I both ordered the same thing. There were two reasons why we ordered that way. We could analyze and discuss the food in more detail and neither one of could wish that she had ordered what the other one was eating. We never shared anything, thinking it was unsanitary and creepy. We both ordered spinach pie as a starter and pastitso for the main course. We would decide on dessert later.

After twin-gramma took the orders in her thick accent I said: "I hope that she gets it right." My eyes went to the ceiling and I put my hands in a position of prayer.

Karen shook her long thick black curls and twisted her mouth before saying: "Should be all right, there's only four things on the menu." We were experts in the field of exaggeration.

I made a theatrical look around and said: "You know with all of these photos, doilies and Greek vases, you would think that this was my grandma's house. It's beginning to freak me out."

"Yeah maybe you're so freaked out that you won't be able to eat."

"Are you kidding? I'll eat even more, like I do when I visit my grandmother. If I didn't have to go there every other Sunday, I would look like Twiggy."

"Yeah, sure, like that's the only place you really eat."

"Not like that. It's a balancing act. If you don't eat enough, which is at least two full plates, you insult her. If you eat too much, my grandmother tells everyone on both sides of the Atlantic that you ate like a pig."

"How do you know how much is just right?"

"You don't. One extra piece of roasted potato could put you over the edge."

We laughed. Karen was just slightly more ladylike that I was.

Just then twin-gramma came over with a whole basket full of dense Greek bread which was the same kind that my grandmother baked every morning. It was hot, fresh and smelled great. Then to our surprise she gave us a big bowl of eggplant spread. I was all excited. There it was, and it wasn't even on the menu.

"It's on the house girls." She smiled as she spoke sounding just like my grandmother.

I could have thanked her in Greek. It was one of the very few words that I knew. Since she gave us something for free, I surmised that she already identified me as a Greek. One Greek word out of me and she would have switched over to Greek entirely and I would be in for it. "What you no speak Greek!" she would say. I must have heard that from random Greeks at least a thousand times since I was born. So, instead I merely said, "Thank you."

The little man from the kitchen came out and looked at us. He seemed pleased to see us digging right in. His face was so ugly and his eyes were so melancholy that his attempt at a smile made him look bizarre.

"Hey Karen, look behind you."

She turned quickly and after seeing him she made a face and said. "Uhg! And to think that he's cooking our food!"

"I know. He's weird. I didn't know there were trolls from Greece."

We laughed and went back to eating and finished it all. It was delicious, just as good as my grandmother's. Maybe she was sharing her recipe with her twin.

"Hey Karen, have you ever wondered why the American kid's grandmothers look like they're 40 while our grandmothers look like they're 80?"

"You're right and the most ridiculous thing is that my grandmother thinks she looks young. If I hear it one more time, 'Look at my skin how beautiful I look. It's the olive oil!', I think I'll stop playing along and tell her what I really think."

"Yeah, I hear the same thing. It looks like the Greek olive oil isn't working any better than the Italian olive oil."

"Do you think that maybe if they dressed like Americans it would make a difference?" Karen asked me.

"You mean like?" I pointed my eyes to twin-gramma. "They could start by switching from black to one of the other 100,000 colors. Our grandmothers certainly could because they're not even widows."

"Yeah and after that maybe buy some panty hose instead of

wearing the stockings rolled up to just under the knee."

"Did you ever wonder how they get those things to stay up? Maybe that's why they don't try to hide their knees. They're showing the world that they can get their stockings to defy gravity."

"Maybe it's the olive oil."

We both laughed again.

"Did I ever tell you that my mother has practically a whole closet filled with lace and embroidered doilies from Greece just like the ones all over this restaurant?" I asked.

"No, I've never seen them at your house. How come?"

"Well grandma keeps sending them to my mother and she would never display such Greekish things around."

That moment twin-gramma brought the food all at once, just like my grandmother did. It smelled fantastic, full of fresh ingredients with the undertones of garlic. I would have liked to be served my spinach pie first, but no matter, everything would be gone soon enough, or so I thought.

Just as I picked up my fork I noticed an embroidered doily on the far wall that looked eerily like the one that I ironed earlier that day. Then I noticed all of the other doilies in great detail. They seemed to be everywhere and circling around me.

My thoughts became so involved with all of these handiworks that my reality seemed to change. The restaurant became darker. Karen seemed farther away. The strange cook who was sitting in the back was staring like he was accusing me of something. Twin-gramma, twin-gramma, I felt guilty calling her that even to myself.

I picked up a fork and thoughts pounced at me from all directions. They came from nearby and from far away; from the present and from and past. I started to eat so as not to alarm Karen or myself. She was busy enjoying her food with her head slightly bend down and her fork moving in a constant rhythm.

The food was delicious, but I felt like I had no right to enjoy it. I didn't tell Karen the real reason why my mother kept the lace and embroidered doilies that she never displayed. She paid for them even though she would never use them.

A lot of fine artistic work went into each one of them by young Greek women who were unmarried and poor with no chances of finding a job. My mother didn't know them but she felt sorry for them. This was one of the few ways that the young women could earn any money at all. So my mother paid for the doilies whenever they were sent to my grandmother. That moment when I looked around the restaurant I could almost see the face of each young woman next to the doily that she crocheted or embroidered; young women with brown hair and brown eyes who must have looked a lot like me. They didn't embroider for fun while listening to the Rolling Stones or while watching television like I did. They didn't put the piece down when they were bored with stitching it. They worked on it until it was finished so they could get a little money from America in order to help their families buy the most basic of food and clothing. I doubted that any one of them had fun on Saturdays like Karen and I did. I doubted any of them would be looking forward to anything more than she already knew.

Then I looked at the cook. Was he really ugly? No, not when I looked at him as a person and not as a subject for my childish judgment and shameful ridicule. I could see that he was a little guy, who probably grew up during World War II when many people in Greece died of hunger. It was clear to me that he had been malnourished. He couldn't help his elf-like appearance. He had a sad face, but a kind one. A little while ago I thought that his smile was grotesque. Now, as I looked through his face, I saw a good, hard working soul. The poor man was smiling because he was glad that we were enjoying his food.   He was smiling because he was happy for us.

I tried to eat now but I was getting light-headed. The lady who owned the restaurant was looking at me with a smile on her now beautiful face. I wondered to myself: "Who was she, what did she leave behind and what sacrifices did she make to get here?"

I then noticed photos of two teenaged boys who were the same ages as my brother and me. Even through their Mediterranean features they looked like tall, healthy and glowing Americans. They were the sons of the little cook.

Then I thought about my grandmother, the one who talked often about missing her village in Greece. Well, I thought, who can blame her. Had the USA really welcomed her? Did she feel a part of anything American? How could she feel when even her own granddaughter was ashamed of her?

My grandmother was only sixteen years old when she came to Brooklyn for an arranged marriage to my grandfather who was then twenty-five years old. When she was my age she already had her first child. That was much harder to deal with than anything that I was doing, and yet for all of these years I made fun of her. She had the courage to come to a land so different from her own that it could have been another planet. Although she never fit in, she had the courage to stay. I hope that she felt satisfaction when she saw her dream come true through the opportunities afforded to her children and even better opportunities for her grandchildren

- opportunities that she could barely understand.

Why hadn't I seen this until today? I shivered as I came out of my reverie and started to move my fork. I ate to celebrate my grandmother's courage. I ate to celebrate that I was embroidering for fun between reading, studying and going out to enjoy myself. I dreamt a wonderful career and a marriage for love and only for love. I wasn't embroidering doilies alone in a dark room, in a bleached white stucco house, in a small island in the Aegean Sea.

The Last Salute

Elizabeth H. Theofan

Today is August 11, 2005, my birthday. It's the big one, 63 years old. Now, why would any normal person think that hitting 63 would be significant? At 60 you start a new decade, at 62 you can start collecting Social Security, and at 65 you can get a half-priced New York Transit System card. But there's one place in the universe, at least in my universe where your 63rd birthday changes everything. It's the mandatory retirement age for everyone employed at the New York City Police Department. In case you are thinking, 'but the Police Commissioner is older than that,' you're right. That's the only exception.

Today is the end of my 40-year career. I'm sitting at my oversized desk. All that is left on it are a telephone and a blotter. My desk drawers are empty, my filing cabinet drawers are empty, my bookcase shelves are empty and my walls are empty. All of my awards, plaques and photographs are in a box at my home in Bay Ridge, Brooklyn. My office is so empty that I can hear an echo when I speak. At least my name is still on the door, Thomas P. Malloy, Chief of Detectives.

It's 10:00AM. I would have been on my way home already, but the Commissioner has orchestrated a final send-off for me which is to take place at noon. So, I'm sitting here with nothing to do and far too much time to think. There is a parade of faces looking into my opened door. When these faces speak I hear: "Hey Chief do you want a cup of coffee?" "Hey Chief can I get you anything?" "Hey Chief would you like me to drive you home?" At least that was something for me to do – guessing what face would appear next and which of the three questions would come out of it. Maybe I should have kept a pad of paper and a pen so that I could keep track of which question was being asked the most.

The first time I heard that there was a mandatory retirement age, I was a 26-year-old Police Officer assigned to the 72nd Precinct in Brooklyn, with three years on the job. That really got me because everyone, and I mean everyone, assigned to the stationhouse knew the exact date they were going to retire and could tell you up to the hour as to how much time they had left. Every single day I heard at least one of my brothers in blue say: "Twenty and out, man that's all I'm doing, not a minute more." So I asked my Sergeant: "Why is there a mandatory retirement age when everyone in this place won't stay a minute beyond the 20 years?" He laughed and then answered while looking at me like he wondered how I could be so smart and so stupid at the same time: "It's not for us. It's for the brass at Headquarters. With the cushy jobs they have, the money they make and with all of us having to kiss their asses, if they didn't have to leave at 63 they would stay forever." After hearing that gem from my Sergeant I suddenly had something I never had before. I had a career path. It was the career path that I would follow all the way to Chief of Detectives.

When I joined the department being a cop was an end in and of itself. I didn't have a college education. It wasn't required back then. I never had that opportunity or ever thought of pursuing it. All I wanted was to be a cop. In my neighborhood the ultimate dream of teenaged boys was to become either a cop or a fireman. My choice was easy. Even from that young age I was a talker, a sociable type. I needed to be around a lot of different types of people. Spending 24 hour shifts with the same bunch of guys in a firehouse wouldn't do it for me. Besides, I didn't know how to cook and had no intention of learning. But most importantly, my inclination was to run away from fire and not into burning buildings.

But I was big, I was brave and maybe a little crazy, but not stupid because I aced every exam up to Captain. From there on, it was all playing politics in order to climb through the levels of Inspector and

Chief to my goal of becoming Chief of Detectives. It helped that since I was a kid I had this sixth sense, second sight, the Dead Zone or whatever. I was like my grandmother who was born and raised in County Conneaut in Ireland. She even saw and spoke with departed spirits and predicted every major family event. What had me convinced was when she predicted the exact date and time of President Kennedy's assassination a full three months before it happened.

Whenever I caught a case, I saw a pathway to its solution very quickly through visions, dreams or hunches. My 95% solution rate was legendary. On the street it was said that I could read minds so the suspects in my cases confessed very quickly. In fact, I helped my fellow detectives out. When they got stuck with a suspect who wouldn't confess they would say: "Do you want us to bring in Malloy?" The suspects couldn't talk fast enough. Consequently, I was given the nickname Nostra-Mc-Damus. At times a derivative of the "F" word was added at the beginning of my nickname as an honorific.

What was even better than my 95% case close-out rate was my 99% kiss ass rate. By using my sixth sense I knew who would help me get my next promotion. I even developed a seventh sense in order to know who was kissing my ass just because he was trying to get something from me. Maybe I'm being too hard on myself because many people in the department are loyal to me. I know that I was a good manager; I sought out talent, shared information and helped many good people get ahead. I played no favorites regarding their ethnic origins. Even though I made sure that they became experts in using the latest data and forensic crime solving tools, I also taught them how to trust and rely on their intuition in solving cases. Since becoming Chief of Detectives ten years ago I more than doubled the number of cases that were closed out, which was unprecedented. Last week a reporter from the New York Times interviewed me and wrote a very complimentary article about how my management style contributed to the   historically high rate of success by the Detective Bureau.

My thoughts were interrupted by another face, an African American face.

"Hey Chief, do you want me to get permission from the 72nd so that your son could drive you home?"

"No, Inspector, I'm good but thanks."

Then it started, thoughts that I didn't want to remember, especially today. But why not today? After all, if I wasn't on the job it never would have happened.

When I became a cop in 1965 the department was predominately Irish, Catholic, and of course, white. Yes, there were a few Black cops but they were up in Harlem. At the 72nd Precinct our diversity consisted of four Italian cops who were always goofing on us, or at least it seemed that way. I have to say that they were great cops who had to put up with a lot of crap from the Irish brass.

It was a different time. The "N" word was used at the stationhouse because most of the cops didn't think there was anything wrong with it. I was no saint but something about using that word always bothered me. I knew very few Black kids, all of them while I was going to public high school. None of them ever did anything bad to me. In fact, I liked them and we got along well, but back then we didn't socialize outside of school. I never used the "N" word, but I am ashamed that I didn't speak up more often when others used it. Meanwhile the cause for civil rights was not being advanced in my own home.   My wife grew up in an all white neighborhood and spent all of her 12 years at a Catholic, all white parochial school. She never even spoke with a Black person. Her father who worked on the docks considered himself an expert on the history of the Black experience in America. When he came to dinner he gave lectures in his thick Irish brogue. One of his favorites was:

"They took our jobs, I tell you."

"What are you talking about? You're working and getting paid quite well, much better than me," I answered.

"Yes, I'm lucky; but when Lincoln freed the slaves they all came up to New York City and took our jobs."

"But you came here from Ireland 80 years after Lincoln signed the Emancipation

Proclamation. And the last I looked all the Irish I know are working. It's the Black guys who have the problems finding jobs."

After these exchanges he would look at me like I was some kind of a lover, and I don't mean a Casanova. This was my world, but in just a few years my world got a lot more colorful.

I was 30 years old, had three children with another on the way. I always had a weakness for kids, loved them all, mine and everyone else's. It was at the end of August. I had made detective 2 years before. Along with my partner we were assigned to take down a major heroin suppler at the Wyckoff Houses in northern Brooklyn, not too far from the Gowanus Canal. We were located on the second floor landing in Staircase A in the southern most building. It must have been 110 degrees and the air smelled like garbage. We had our guns drawn. There were shots ringing out above. The drug kingpin had been tipped off somehow that we were coming for him. Just then I sensed something, someone moving on the stairs. Thank God that my Irish magic clicked in. I swear that I was able to see through the underside of the metal staircase. I screamed to my partner – "Joe don't shoot......It's a kid." Just as I said "kid" I saw his face. It was a Black boy about 9 years old, the same age as my oldest son. He was skinny and scared seeing these two big white guys with guns. "Come here son, don't be afraid." I shouted to him but tried to take the edge off of my voice as I added: "Get behind us now!" I was shaking. If it wasn't for the angels or whatever gave me x-ray vision either Joe or I may have killed the kid. One minute later our back-up arrived and we let them take over.

We were no good just then. The only thing to do was to take the boy outside. The boy was looking down at the pavement as if he were ashamed; as if he did something wrong.

"What's your name?" I asked, but there was no answer.

"What's your name?" There was still no answer.

"We're not strangers. We're your friends. We're police."

"Winston, my name is Winston.

"Where do you live Winston? We'll take you there."

"There," and he pointed to the building that was about 50 feet north from where we were standing.

"Hey Joe, I'll take him." I noticed that Joe looked worse than I felt so I left him standing there and walked off with Winston.

Just then the boy looked up and directly at me. I was stunned. Winston looked familiar, like his face belonged somewhere in my family. Incredibly, as a shock against his light brown skin, he had blue eyes, just a shade darker than mine. As we locked eyes I could see the tension leaving the boy, as if he recognized me.

I asked him: "Winston, what were you doing in that building?"

"I was visiting a friend from Sunday School."

"Why didn't you take the elevator down?"

"It's always broken."

He stopped walking, paused and asked, "What's your name mister policeman, sir?"

I chuckled a bit, "My name is Tommy."

"That was my father's name."

"What's your last name Winston?"

"It's Mara."

Well I thought, that could explain a lot. We resumed walking. A few minutes later we were on the elevator. Thankfully, at least this one was working. It was way too hot to climb up the stairs. We got off on the 4th Floor and rang the bell at apartment 4C.

I wasn't ready for my whole world to change. But, who ever is? Winston's mother opened the door. Over the years I have thought about this moment thousands of times. The most beautiful woman who ever walked the earth opened the door. I'm 6'2" tall and back then I weighed 220 pounds of pure muscle. She was almost as tall as I was and no less than 40 pounds under what I weighed. Her beautiful face with her brown complexion was glowing. It was flawless without one mark on it. Her skin was perfect. She was wearing a sundress with a tropical print that fit and flattered her voluptuous curves perfectly. Her hair was thick, worn up and perfect. She wore gold hoop earrings with a floral design along with a matching necklace and bracelet, which were perfect. Her high heeled sandals were multicolored and the way they matched her dress was perfect. She was perfect.

This may sound corny. This may sound trite. But I swear that her large, and couldn't be darker brown eyes held all of the secrets of the universe. Even before we spoke I knew that no matter what we would ever talk about that I would defer to her, because her powers were stronger than mine. I have never, before or since, felt that way about anyone else.

I was glad that she spoke first because for the first time in my life I was speechless. "Hello detective. My name is Mrs. Patrice Mara.

Thank you for saving my son's life."

I didn't ask her how she knew. I wonder about it until this day. Did someone tell her or had she seen it in a vision?

"My name is Tommy Malloy and you are very welcome." I answered while sounding lame and standing there like a dork.

"Won't you come in and sit down?"

"Thank you, Mrs. Mara."

"Please call me Patrice."

"Please call me Tommy."

I sat down in a very plush comfortable chair.

"Please relax, Tommy, I'll be right back."

She escorted her son to his room. I could hear her consoling him. Her voice was incredible, clear as a bell with a lilting Caribbean accent.

She came back a while later with tea and coconut bread, on a very fancy tray with a china kettle, cups and plates to match. This was my first foray into unknown foods, at least unknown to me. Patrice was at the helm leading me on. The coconut bread was delicious.

"Is it homemade?"

"Yes, I baked it this morning."

We sat and talked for two hours telling each other all about ourselves. She was a registered nurse and a midwife. In her profession she was surrounded with new life while I investigated destruction and death. She was saving every penny she could in order to move out of the projects and to buy her own home. Her apartment, at least of what I saw of it, was arranged beautifully. She did all of her own decorating, and sewed her slipcovers and curtains. In addition, she was an accomplished clothes designer and tailor. She saved even more money by sewing all of her and her son's clothes without the use of patterns.

She anticipated my biggest question. After all Winston had spoken about his father in the past tense. Patrice told me that she was a widow. She had only one child, Winston, whose 9th birthday just passed at the beginning of the month. The three of them used to live in Kingston, Jamaica. Her husband was a decorated police detective who was shot and killed during a drug bust. This happened three years before. Her husband's name was Tommy Mara. His father was pure Irish and his mother, a half-white Jamaican woman. She told me that other than the difference of skin color and my slightly lighter blue eyes that my face and build were exactly like her late husband's.

She told me that she was concerned about Winston. He had been withdrawn since his father was killed. He preferred to spend time reading alone in his room to playing with other boys. His only friend was Billy, the boy who he was visiting in the next building. Billy was a very good, smart and religious boy but he was a loner just like Winston. Patrice was proud of

Winston. He got good grades in school but she knew that much more was needed for him to succeed in the world. Patrice was concerned that unless her son learned how to get along with all kinds of people, he would never fulfill his God given potential. He needed the influence of a man who was respected like his late father. All of her relatives were still in Jamaica so his uncles could not be of any help. She had to get away from all of the bad and sad memories so she moved to Brooklyn. I said that I would help.

Then I took her telephone number and left.

I was true to my word. For the next year I took Winston out at least twice a month, sometimes every week. It was clear that Winston was extremely bright and he was also very perceptive. He had the ability to recall minute details of every place we ever visited and everything we did together. It was a pleasure to be with him. He behaved like a little man, never asking for anything or complaining. He was appreciative of whatever we did together. We went mostly to Prospect Park to play catch or to watch the Puerto Rican pick-up baseball games. Sometimes I took him to the amusement parks in Coney Island, sometimes to the movies, once to the Museum of Natural History and once to the Police Museum at the Academy. But Winston's favorite place to go was Shea Stadium so that he could see his Mets. I took him a few times but I was only able to afford the seats in the upper tier. Winston didn't mind, as long as he was there.

At the end of each day with Winston we were treated to a cooked from scratch dinner created by Patrice. All three of us would dine and talk. Her conversation was more serious while I would occasionally crack jokes. But, there was a limit of how many of them that Patrice would tolerate. Everything she said or did had a purpose. One evening, I confided in them that someday I wanted to become the Chief of Detectives. Frequently, after Patrice's subtle prompting, Winston would ask thoughtful and probing questions about the NYPD. She would add her own morality tales about the police doing God's work. Patrice was able to incorporate Bible verses into these conversations seamlessly.

I told no one about Patrice or Winston. My wife and her family never know. My hours had been so crazy for so many years that they built a life without me. My fellow detectives suspected that something was up. Maybe one to them saw me with Winston. Maybe one of them followed me. Who knows and who cares? They never had to nerve to ask. But they were funny. One day I found a big coconut on my desk. A bunch of them were standing around to see my reaction. I looked at my coconut like it had always been there and immediately started using it as a paperweight. A week later I found a small Jamaican flag on my desk. The flag was three by four inches with a six-inch pole and a three-inch diameter base. I hollered out: "Does anyone here have any glue?" I never saw men move so fast. I heard drawers opening and closing and a whole bunch of voices hollering: "Where's the glue?" I knew these guys would find it even if they had to go out and buy it themselves. Ten minutes later I glued the flag base onto the coconut. That was the end of my "gifts."

I fell in love with Patrice, a love that I never thought possible let alone thought that I would ever experience. I was in awe of her, I admired her and I respected her. I never visited her apartment when she was alone. I never went out with her. I never even touched her even though I often thought about what that would be like. Nevertheless, I felt guilty. In many ways this was even worse that a physical affair because I gave her my heart. I also loved Winston like he was my own child.

At home I was known as a fussy eater. I wouldn't eat my

wife's stew if there was lamb in it.
She had to make it with beef. Her
father would carry on, "Are you
sure he's Irish? He likes English
stew I tell you!" I wouldn't even try
brussel sprouts. Her father – he
seemed to always be there – would
say, "For Christ sake, Tommy. If
you can eat a cabbage you can eat a
sprout. What do you think it is but
a wee cabbage?"

But when I was eating dinner
with Patrice and Winston, I gladly
ate things that I had never seen,
smelled or tasted before. I didn't
ask what was in them. That would
have made me feel like I was

betraying my wife even more. I wouldn't eat her lamb at home but here I was taking seconds of curried goat or oxtail stew and heaven knows what else.

About a year after I befriended Winston I saved up and was able to buy box seats at Shea Stadium to give him a special treat for his 10th birthday. I was all excited about how happy Winston would be when I called Patrice.

"Hi, it's me, Tommy."

"Hello Tommy." She sounded different, serious, and distant.

"Anything wrong?"

"No, Tommy."

"Well OK. I have a special surprise for Winston. For his birthday, guess what?   I got box seats for Shea Stadium!"

"He won't be going Tommy."

"Why, is he sick?"

"No he's fine."

"Then does he have somewhere else to go?"

"No, Tommy."

"Then what is it?"

"We both have to say goodbye to you now, Tommy."

I knew that it was final.

"But why?"

"Because last night Winston asked me if you were his new father."

"Can't you say that I'm an uncle?" That sounded stupid. I knew what she was saying. I had been anticipating this conversation for a while. That's why I had gotten the expensive tickets. I felt that the end was coming. I wanted to give Winston one last big treat.

"Tommy, you know better."

"But how will you explain to him why I'm not coming to see him anymore? What will you tell him?"

"The truth."

Now that had me stumped and speechless. After allowing me a minute to wonder Patrice went on.

"I will tell him that you were sent to us for a while as a result of his father's prayers in heaven. You were sent here to save his life and to make sure that he was on the right path. So, your work is done and you have other children to help. Winston and I will go to church and thank Jesus for you being in our lives for this past year."

"I understand. I wish both of you the best. I just have one question and it's very selfish. You see things, I know you do. Will I be safe on the job?"

"Oh yes, Tommy, you will have a magnificent 40-year career and you will become Chief of Detectives."

"One more question, please."

"OK Tommy, ask it."

"Will I ever find out what happens to Winston?"

"You will, but not for many years."

"Again Patrice I wish you all the best. You are the finest, most beautiful person I have ever met." I knew better than to tell her that I loved her.

"Goodbye, Tommy."

And that was it, the last time I ever spoke with Patrice. I never saw her again. Years later, I found out that she moved out of the Wyckoff houses. Although I could have found her very easily, I never tried. As a young man full of love and passion I was afraid that I would pursue her. In addition, that would have ruined my relationship with Winston. As a mature man I realized that some things in life are best left in their time. But, for a span of almost 20 years I checked the lists of new police recruits to see if Winston Mara's name was on them. I stopped checking when he would have been too old to qualify. I hoped that because of my influence, he would have joined the NYPD. Today he would be 42 years old, the same age as I was when I was promoted to full Inspector.

Just then, mercifully, another face appeared at my doorway.

"Chief, the Commissioner will be here in 10 minutes."

"Thank you!" I smiled and waved.

This was to be my last meeting with the Commissioner. No longer would I have to sit through his weekly three-hour staff meetings. I loved him but hated his meetings. He was always 10 to 20 minutes late. That's when I would have to listen to 19 other old men talk about their ailments – knee surgery, hip replacements, bad backs, heart attacks, stints, diabetes, acid reflux and a detailed description of all corresponding treatments and medication. There were four women who regularly attended these meetings. They were far more macho than the men. I never heard one health complaint from any of them. Each week it was the same. If there was a male guest at the meeting invariably he would join in and maybe, we would have the privilege of hearing about a brand new medical condition.

One day I finally had enough. I said: "Since all you men are talking about your health and because I am very concerned I would like to take a survey." The room went quiet as they all stared at me thinking: Now what! "Is there anyone here who takes Viagra?" At least there was some masculine pride still left at the topmost management level at the NYPD. They all shut up. A minute later the Commissioner, used to a loud buzz in the room when he entered to start his staff meeting, looked puzzled by the dead silence.

Then there it was - the last face that would appear in my doorway. It was the same face that appears in a framed photograph in every NYPD precinct house and in every NYPD office in the City of New York. In my doorway was the face of the Police Commissioner, himself. The Commissioner had been wonderful to me. He left me alone to do my job and in exchange, I always gave him the glory. He appreciated me so much that he orchestrated my one of a kind send-off.

I rose as he walked into the office. He smiled as he came over and shook my hand.

"Hey Chief, you lucky dog, in a few minutes you'll be free. Starting tomorrow you will be collecting more money than you are making now." He was right. That's how our pensions work after 40 years. "Have you decided which of the three jobs you'll be taking?"

I had gotten job offers to be the head of security from three different international corporations, but at this point all I wanted was to take a long vacation to travel with my family and think about my next life.

"No Commissioner, not yet. I don't even know if I want another job after this."

"Well, with your abilities you could always hang out a shingle on the side of you house and do fortune telling."

We both laughed. Just then I heard the bagpipes tuning-up.

"So Commissioner, who is coming out to take part in this send-off?"

"Just about everyone will be there, first your detectives, then the uniform bureau chiefs and precinct commanders and finally one high ranking police representative from each of Rockland, Westchester, Suffolk, and Nassau counties."

"Why would any police from the other counties be there? I haven't worked with any of them for years."

"They're not only paying tribute to you, Chief Malloy the man. They're paying tribute to the legend, to the great Notra-Mc-Damus."

We both laughed again.

"By the way, what's this I hear about you not wanting a ride home?"

Him too!

"No Commissioner, from the subway I cameth into this life and to the subway I leaveth this life."

"OK, have it your way," he said as he rolled his eyes and smiled.

"It's hot; we shouldn't keep them waiting any longer. Are you ready for your final tribute?"

"I am and I am honored. But before we go out there, Commissioner, I would like to thank you for everything. You made it easy for me to do my job."

"No, thank you, Chief. You made me look good. You're the best

Chief of Detectives that this department has ever had, and I mean ever."

After 40 years of listening to a lot of talk I wanted these to be the last words I heard as I left my former office and until I left the building.

We walked out in silence and after a few steps, got on his private elevator. We then walked across the mercifully deserted lobby and out the front door of Police Headquarters.

The pipers were playing on either side of us as we walked out onto the plaza. It was sunny and hot. I could hear the cheering even over the drone of the pipes. The Commissioner then hung back and said: "It's your show, Chief, enjoy it."

Everyone was lined up along the north side of the wide walkway of Police Plaza. The loudest noise came from my detectives who were clapping, whistling and hollering. I was so proud of them although they were quite a sight. None of them were dressed in uniform. They wore summer casual or outrageous street clothing. There were men and women, tall and short. It was a sea of faces of different shapes and skin tones. They were not like the white Irish and few Italian masculine faces that I saw 40 years ago. Every ethnic group was represented; it was as if the entire city turned-out to honor me.

I walked up to and faced each person. Each of them saluted me first, and after exchanging a few words, I saluted back. As I was going through the line I relived many of my most important moments – some sad and some funny. Everyone who worked on the biggest cases with me since I became Chief of Detectives was there. Some of them had already retired. I continued to move along the line reaching the NYPD uniform brass. These were the guys that I "grew up" with as we rose in the department together. There was plenty of talking and laughter. Finally, I got to the police representatives of each of the four counties closest to New York City. First came Rockland, then Westchester, then Suffolk and then there was a gap.

I had to walk a few more steps before I reached the officer in his dress uniform from Nassau County. I stood right in front of him. He saluted me. It was as if I were seeing myself through a smoky lens of a time machine. He was exactly my height and had the same build that I had 20 years ago. I looked into his face but for the skin tone, two decades ago it could have been my face. His blue eyes were a shade darker than mine. I didn't need to read his name tag to know who he was but I looked anyway. It read Winston T. Mara, Inspector.

"Thank you for everything Chief, sir," was all that he said.

I touched his arm and answered, "The pleasure was always mine, Inspector."

I then stood at attention as I looked directly at Winston and I gave him the last salute.

It was finished.

Halfway on my way to the subway I tasted something salty as a tear fell into my smile.

Happily Ever After?
(the road is long, with many a winding turn)
Joyce Webster-O'Rourke

The warm, highly polished, wood floor framed a thick, beige and burgundy paisley rug.

An oval mahogany coffee table, in the center, held a large scallop shell, several small geodes and a box of tissues. Three paintings, impressionistic seascapes, decorated the creamy walls and a single wide window opened to a view of the Verrazano Bridge and the sea beyond it. Two small sofas, some throw pillows, a couple of end tables, lamps and an oversized wing chair comfortably filled the room and conveyed an aura of peaceful invitation and welcome.

Jimmy, however, was feeling none of that. He was sitting, stonily, barely breathing, in a corner of one of the love seats, as far away as he could get from the chair and the sandy-haired man who sat in it. His body ached with tension and his head felt as if it would burst if he did not get out of there. Forthwith. How had it come to this? What was he, Jimmy Sullivan, doing, sitting in a

shrink's office, his life in a
shambles? Twenty years ago, he
was twenty-one, had a dream job in
the dot com world, earned a six
figure salary and got great bonuses.
He dropped out of college and, in
1994, he and Patty were married.
Her brother, Billy, was his best man.
He had been Jimmy's idol since he
met saw him on the basketball
court when he was a kid. Billy was a
senior at Ford and captain of the
basketball team; he liked to teach
the "little" kids how to play. Jimmy's
sister, Meghan and Billy were
married in1990. Four years later,
she was radiantly pregnant at his

own wedding, a beautiful matron of honor. The wedding was in St. Francis

Xavier, in Park Slope, the reception was at the Prospect Hall. Emerald Society pipers played at the church and the reception. They hired *Alive N Kickin* as their band and they honeymooned in Ireland.

Everything was story-book perfect and they looked forward to happily ever after.

His mind wandered. "Most men lead lives of quiet desperation." *Who the hell said that? Oh yeah, Thoreau. Not me,* had been his reaction when they discussed it in a lit class at Saint John's University. *Not me, not ever.* It seemed a million years ago. But, here he was, in 2009. *An angry, middle-aged, alcoholic, suspended cop whose wife fled him eight years ago. She said she was terrified of him; he had laughed at her then, but hell, he was afraid of himself, of the man he had become.*

The shrink shifted slightly; his movement brought Jimmy's attention back into the room.

Christ, he thought, how long have I been sitting here? Mute as a megalith and almost as still? He looked at his watch. Forty-five minutes! He made eye contact with the shrink and quickly looked away.

"This time is yours, Jimmy," John said. "You came for many reasons, not the least of which is your wish to get your job back. How you use our time together is up to you. How can I help?

Jimmy glared at him; words stuck in his throat. Finally he said: "I'm out of here."

"Okay, your next appointment is Thursday at noon."

"Stuff it up your ass" he yelled as he slammed the door.

John finished his session notes and closed the laptop. *Can Jimmy, will Jimmy, accept help and do the hard but necessary work to get his life back on track?* John wouldn't bet on it, either way.

Thursday, Jimmy was there, on time.

John opened the door and waved Jimmy to a seat. He sat in the same corner and stared out the window. The Verrazano was shrouded in fog but he could see emergency vehicles on the lower level. *Wonder what's going on*, he thought.

"How are you, today, Jimmy?"

"FINE." *Stupid shrink. What am I supposed to say?*

A long silence followed. Jimmy twisted inside with helplessness and frustration. Finally , he growled, "I don't know what to say or how to do this."

"It's hard to talk about yourself but you're clearly feeling something intense right now. You could begin with that and see where it goes."

Silence. Jimmy made eye contact, defiant and prolonged. He leaned forward. "Okay. I'm pissed off. I don't belong here. I can manage my own life. You're no better than me. Who the hell are you, anyway, to sit in judgment of me? To decide when I can go back to work?"

"Jimmy, the department says you're unfit for duty, yet they clearly feel that you're salvageable. I'm here to help you if you want it. You're free to refuse my assistance. There's no particular way to do this. Just talk about whatever runs through your head."

The sun broke through the fog and the blinking lights rolled off the bridge. "Whatever, you say? All right then. I had it all. Seemed like I had the Midas touch; everything I did made money. My company survived the beginning of the dot com disaster in the late nineties. Patty and I are cautious people with simple tastes. We lived well but conservatively. So we had saved and invested. Some of my friends were not so lucky; they thought the easy money would go on forever. A college buddy committed suicide, leaving two small children. Walt had been living high; he had no insurance and no savings. Patty and I provided some emotional support for his widow and some practical stuff. We helped her find a smaller home and get her financial life in order."

Jimmy paused, brushing his hand across his forehead. "We talked about our own options. The handwriting was on the wall and I was kind of done with that world, anyway. Ready for a second career, at twenty-six," he laughed. "We had more money than we would ever need. When I was a kid, I wanted to be a cop, you know, have the gun, the cuffs, catch the bad guys. I took the test, aced it and started in the academy in 1997."

He stopped talking, picked up a geode and ran his hand over its smooth face. He glanced at the shrink, waiting for him to comment. *Bastard! Just sits there, like the goddamn Sphinx. How is his life? Does he even have one? Is there anyone he cares about, anyone he loves? He seems like a cold son of a bitch.* Jimmy was suddenly exhausted, mind and body craving sleep. He put the geode down and leaned back. He could not sleep here. He stood up abruptly, and moved to the door. "I need to go, right now."

"Okay. Jimmy, you've made a good start. Be gentle with yourself but pay attention to your feelings this weekend. See you Tuesday, same time."

John sighed and smiled wryly. *Jimmy is one smart guy; Wish I had some of his acumen. The money wouldn't hurt either. What happened to send him over the edge?*

*

The exhaustion stayed with Jimmy on the drive home but as he eased the car into the garage, remorse and regret rose in his mind and thoughts of sleep receded. *Patty.* He had kept the house.

She wanted nothing to do with it and would not accept any financial help from him. She lived in a tiny apartment in Carroll Gardens and, from what he heard, was doing well. She enjoyed her work at the Administration for Children's Services, saw her friends, called his mother a couple of times a week and saw her on Saturdays when she went to see the girls She took their nieces to soccer games and ballet classes and arranged special treats for them. Tea parties at American

Girl when they were younger; now shows and concerts. As far as he knew, she did not date; his mother refused to answer questions about Patty, beyond saying that she was well. He still called once a week but she did not answer his calls. His message was always the same: "Patty, I love you and miss you. I'm so sorry I hurt you."

He opened the refrigerator; nothing but juice, milk, some non-alcoholic beer (*disgusting stuff*) and water. He let the door swing shut. His body ached for a Chivas Regal and his psyche teased, *just one won't hurt.* It was now five days since his last drink. *Well, four days, seventeen hours and thirty-five minutes.* It was the hardest thing he had ever done. He changed his clothes and hit the treadmill in the basement. Forty punishing minutes later, he showered and dressed. Still too early to meet his friends for dinner and the ballgame. He watered Patty's plants, puttered around, then got a bottle of water and sat in the recliner. *Christ, I'm bored. I have to get out of here.*

He got up quickly and got into the car. He drove along the Belt Parkway to Rockaway Parkway and walked to the fence by the water.

Memories, like ghosts, taunted him. Patty, Meghan, Billy, all gone from his life. September 11, 2001 had changed everything. Meghan never made it down from her office in Tower I and Billy perished with a couple of hundred other firefighters. *Jesus Christ, what a waste.* He stopped going to church and began to worship the bottle. It gave him no comfort but it obliterated the past-- as long as he stayed drunk.

Patty mourned in her own way; she threw herself into caring for Meghan's and Billy's little girls and easing other peoples' pain. He just shut her out. He came home from work one night in 2002 to find Patty, the dog and her clothes gone. A cryptic note told him she loved him, told him to get help and to leave her alone until he did. "Love? You bitch," he had shouted. He threw the kitchen chairs around, smashed a couple of plants, and finished a bottle of Chivas Regal and a few bottles of beer. He woke up the next morning on the kitchen floor, soaked in his own pee and vomit. He shook his head to banish the memories and went to meet his friends.

*

Jimmy arrived promptly twice a week for the next three weeks. He complained but he followed the regimen John outlined for him, meditating, journaling, exercising, and so on. Between sessions he paid attention to his feelings, thoughts and dreams and discussed them with John. There was one exception. He did not talk of Patty or tell the shrink that she had left him. In the fifth week of therapy, John questioned him directly about his marriage. Jimmy responded with angry evasions but John persisted. Finally, Jimmy screamed, "All right, she left me years ago. Took the dog and beat it. Happy now?" He did not wait for a response from John. On the way home he bought a couple of bottles of Chivas Regal and some Jamisons for good measure.

He didn't just fall off the wagon. He catapulted. He was drunk, unshaven and belligerent when he showed up on Tuesday. John told him to take the train home and to come to his next appointment sober. Jimmy stormed out, got into his car, drove a few blocks and got a ticket for driving under the influence. "God damned fucking shrink."

John finished his notes and his own memories engulfed him. He had started drinking at thirteen. It eased the pain of his father's death and helped him overcome his shyness and insecurity. Somehow, he managed to keep his grades up and only Joe knew about it; his older brother drank more than he did so it really didn't matter. Then Joe died and he drank steadily. *I was lucky. Father Fox saw the road I was headed down and he helped me turn around, took me to his AA meetings and mentored me clear through grad school. It's a hell of a battle. I hope Jimmy is able to make it.*

*

The next morning, sober and contrite, Jimmy called for help. John faxed him a list of AA meeting places and times. Angry that John would not see him until his regular appointment, Jimmy balled the message up and threw it in the trash. *Why should I meet with a bunch of losers? Why?* His bleary-eyed image in the mirror mocked him. He fished the list out of the trash and chose a meeting out in Nassau County, figuring no one there would recognize him. With support, he was able to stay drug and alcohol free.

*

On a blustery March morning, a Tuesday, eight months after he joined AA , Jimmy entered the office and sat on the sofa nearest the chair. He had long since ceased to think of John as a "shrink."

John looked at him steadily. "Jimmy, you've done good work here. Your anger and hostility have eased. You've been sober for six months and you're taking responsibility for your actions. I think you're ready to go back to work; light duty for a while. See how it goes."

Conflicting emotions raged in Jimmy. Panic...*Don't cut me loose now, when I am learning so much and feeling so much better.* Elation...*I really am better!* Still, he was no way sure that he was ready. He had come to rely on these sessions to help him sort through his pain.

John smiled. "You can continue to come, once a week, to work on your other issues but you're no longer self-destructive or dangerous to others."

Relief flooded through Jimmy; tears flowed down his cheeks. He could go back to work! He could still try to resolve his conflicts and put his life back together.   He wanted to hug John but settled for shaking his hand, vigorously.

The next week was a disaster and the session with John was discouraging.   He wanted to talk about getting Patty back but John wanted to hear about his days at work. *Sometimes, John, you can be a real prick.* They were crappy and Jimmy did not want to focus on them. People were wary of him; no one seemed to trust him. He felt like a pariah.

"Uh, you could talk about that," John's voice intruded on his thoughts and Jimmy realized he had spoken out loud.

"Fuck it! I don't want to think about work; I want to figure out how I can get Patty back," he spat out, glaring. A long and, for Jimmy, very uncomfortable silence ensued. He stared at the largest geode, a swirl of blues, aqua, sky and royal, highly polished and beautiful, imprisoned in a rough, gray and tan coating. He picked it up, then focused his blue, tear-filled eyes on John. "I don't think I can do it," his voice was barely audible as he set the geode down and drew back into the sofa. He grabbed a throw pillow and held it tightly against his body.

John waited. He gazed out the window and back to Jimmy. "Let it out."

Jimmy shook his head; he punched the pillow and tossed it aside. "They don't like me...don't want me there...people always liked me. I'm a fun guy.. I'm a good friend. Now though, they treat me with kid gloves, like I'm breakable or, oh I don't know, like a container of nitro." Silence. He looked up and grinned sheepishly as he suddenly realized why that was. "I guess it's going to take time-and work-and patience."

John chuckled and nodded.

Jimmy took the cue. "I've told you some of what I did. There's a lot more. I was doing one night stands with prostitutes. Once, they sent me a kid. Really a kid! I found out later she was fifteen. I wanted to help her. Her pimp was a drug dealer, Irish and Puerto Rican, as smart and as vicious as they come. CC he called himself; I had busted him a couple of times and copped some of his stash. He didn't like me much. Anyway, this kid reminded me of

Meghan and I couldn't give up on her. I was afraid to talk to her myself. I knew he would hurt her if he found out. I had this friend, a woman I knew from the academy. She tried to help the girl. CC must have found out. He shot the girl up with God knows what and watched her seizing in the snow in Dumbo. He did it again and again. Finally, someone saw her and called 911. The kid lived but her mind is gone and her right side is paralyzed. She's a vegetable. I went ballistic. Went to his place, trashed it, beat the shit out of a couple of his people but never found him. My partner tried to stop me and I pointed my gun at him. He put in for a change. That was partner number one. Three more followed and here I am. Being here, this therapy thing, has been an unbelievable journey but the guys at the precinct have no way of knowing I am...uh...whole again." He was quiet for a few minutes. He shook his head and began again. "I was a mess. I would go home after a day of picking up and manhandling perps. I was disgusting and disgusted. With the world, with humanity, with myself. I drank myself stupid every night so I could sleep, so the nightmares couldn't start, so the ghosts couldn't come. Then the alcohol wasn't enough. I roughed up a few dealers and then offered to protect them when I could. I had a fairly steady supply but I needed more and more." He threw the pillow down." I can't talk anymore. I got worse; don't want to think about it." He stood up and left without looking at John.

Rough session! Something seems about to break through. John reached for his laptop.

Thursday morning, Jimmy slumped into the office, avoiding eye contact. He toyed with the geodes

and picked up the smallest, a swirl
of purples, grays and ghostly whites.
He ran his fingers over its cold,
smooth finish. "I...I did some really
sick things. Horrible things." Tears
rolled down his cheeks and he
lapsed into silence.

After a few minutes, John
leaned forward. "Can you talk about
it, Jimmy?"

"I did...the prostitutes...there
was one..." He looked away.

A long silence. "It seems
important, Jimmy."

"I was working undercover, in
Dumbo, and...Oh God...I can't...I was

so angry... Black eyes, waist length, straight hair, skin the color of very light coffee...and huge breasts. She wore a short, loose, white, lace, blousy thing. She flipped it up as I went by. There was nothing under it. I turned and grabbed her breast; it was warm and hard. She took me to a basement in an abandoned building. I pulled her clothes off, threw her on the filthy mattress and started sucking her. John, I never did that before; I always only wanted the sex. Anyway, I got a mouthful of warm, weird, stuff. I spit it out. A nursing mother! I was furious. I stood up, dropped my pants and rode her until I was exhausted. Then...I emptied her, slowly at first, then faster and harder.

Finally, I lay there with her breast filling my mouth; I was crying. After a while, she got up, I paid her and we left. I went back for her every day, for months. How sick is that? With her, it wasn't the sex. I craved the feel of her breast in my mouth, the trickle of the milk as it slid down my throat...total relaxation, peace. I needed her...and I hated her...because of the baby. She had no right. I had no right. I got rougher each time. Then one night when I went for her, she was gone. The guys in the bar said the Cow moved uptown." He could not look at John.

John handed him a box of tissues.

"About a year later, I was working out of Sunset Park. I saw her with a little boy. He looked to be about four years old. I wanted her...I blocked her way and reached for her. She put her arm across her breasts and looked at me with cold, dead eyes. In that moment, I was afraid of her. What kind of animal am I? Her kid was there...how could I even think about taking her then...how low can I be? But John, if

I saw her again, and she was alone...I'd do the same thing again." He stood up and headed toward the door.

"Sit down, Jimmy. Don't go yet; this is crucial. Your moment of truth as it were; not something to shrink from. You've clearly been through a part of hell. Your need, your anger, have roots that go back much further than the prostitute. Your guilt and remorse are healthy. Your self-loathing is not." John paused. "Have you been meditating?"

"I try...I'm no good at it."

"Still, I'd like you to try some focused meditation this weekend. Imagine yourself as a very young child. Feel, be, the small, possibly pre-verbal toddler that you were. What were the   sounds, smells, tastes and sights that surrounded you? Who were the people in your life? What made you happy, sad, angry, comfortable and so on. Let the thoughts flow. Write them down whenever you can. Do this at least three times a day. It will be hard, painful work. If you get into trouble or feel overwhelmed, you can call me. See you Tuesday.

John's neck and shoulders ached. He stood up, stretched and looked out the window. The sky and water were varying shades of pewter. Ordinarily he loved this kind of day but today it seemed to press in on him. *All way the years of study, observation, reflection and I am still amazed at how quickly a good human being can slip down the path to depravity. And how difficult it can be to find the way back. God go with you, Jimmy.*

*

Jimmy's face was drawn, his shoulders slumped and his steps heavy when he came in on Tuesday.

374

"Look, I got nothing. Just my Da, lilting an Irish tune and dancing around the kitchen, with me in his arms. Nice memory, right? Didn't feel like it though."

"How did it feel?

"Lonely, sad---I felt little, weak, afraid and so---alone. That's it.

"That's good work, Jimmy. See if you can fill in some of the details. What color was the kitchen? Who else was there? Did your father do things like that often? What were the sounds, smells, sights? Take your time. Use your breathing routine to relax."

He shook his head and stared at the floor. Finally, tight-voiced: "Meghan was at the table, doing homework, I think. She had to be six or seven so I was...maybe two." Then,   explosively: "I was a baby for God's sake, what could I possibly know? *What is the matter with this fucking shrink?* You have all the answers and you won't help me." He sat back and glared.

"Jimmy, you do know something important...something that was buried and is struggling to come into your awareness." John leaned forward, forcing Jimmy' to look at him. "And while I *do* have theoretical knowledge and some thoughts, conjectures really, about what happened, I *do not* know *your* experience. And I don't want to influence or mislead you. What I think won't help you right now; only you can do this work."

Minutes passed. Jimmy hugged a pillow to his chest, closed his eyes and drew several deep breaths. "Maybe the day I'm thinking about is the day the twins came home. My mother was nursing them and I had the mother of all tantrums. My father took me out of the room and tried to calm me down. I guess...maybe I was...jealous." He bit his lips. He stood up, went to the window and stood so his back was to John. "You son of a bitch...was that what you want?"

John sighed. "Wrong question, Jimmy. What do you want? What did the sad, angry and lonely baby want? And what is the sad, angry and lonely man looking for?"

"My mother's breasts?...That's really twisted, even for a shrink."

"It was completely normal for a two year old."

"I have to get out of here. I feel like puking."

"This isn't easy, Jimmy. Pay attention to the little boy in you. I think his feelings were natural and strong but they weren't accepted. So they were buried and have festered all these years. But you need to see for yourself if it's true for you. Keep digging and come in Thursday.

*

Jimmy drove along the BQE, heading to his AA meeting. Traffic was a mess so he got off in Willliamsburg. Suddenly his mouth

379

was dry, his pulse racing. Images of the Cow invaded his thoughts. *Oh Christ. I want her.* In Queens, he parked in front of a bar; a cop hangout on Greenpoint Avenue. He ordered a shot of Jamison's and a pint of Harp. The guy next to him was drinking black coffee. *Shit...I want...* He pushed the drinks away and ordered coffee, to go. He got through the night and the next day with support from his sponsor, agonizing exercise, mediation and writing. His sleep was roiled by dreams of his parents, the Cow, Patty and Meghan. To his disgust, he woke up several times with his

fingers in his mouth. Thursday
morning, he was in John's office
early. He rambled on about the
dreams and his childhood, carefully
avoiding the thing that was really
on his mind.

"All right, Jimmy, let's have it."

"I get the feeling that you
don't think I did anything
wrong...that I couldn't help it. I don't
buy that crap. You know...the devil
made me do it stuff."

"No way. I can't give you a
pass on your behavior. It was
wrong, according to law, to your
oath as a police officer, to your

religious beliefs and probably, most of all, to your understanding of human relations. That said, when you described your meetings with the prostitutes, especially with the Cow, there *was* a compulsive quality to it. That needs to be explored."

Jimmy looked away. "From the first time I touched her, I felt like she was mine, mine; I couldn't let her go. It was weird...ecstatic...dreamy. The feel of her filling my mouth...the milk responding to my suck...oh my God...it's true, isn't it?" He gnawed at his thumb. "You were right. My mother gave my brothers what was mine, mine, mine." When his sobs subsided, Jimmy began to put pieces into place. His long-buried anger at his mother for giving his brothers her/his milk---his need for and anger at the Cow for giving away what belonged to her baby. "It does make sense, John. So that's it, it's done?"

"That part, Jimmy."

Slowly, Jimmy began to heal.

*

He spent the next couple of sessions re-hashing his childhood, connecting events and consequences. He was fascinated by psychology but became bogged down in his own minutia. John interrupted a long monologue: "Time to talk about where you want to go from here, Jimmy."

Grabbing a pillow, Jimmy shrunk deeply into the couch.

John watched. "Notice what you did there, Jimmy."

"Nothing. I'm just sitting here. You mean the pillow? Shit."

Nodding, John said: "Mmm, you do that when you feel threatened, or when you're avoiding something and don't want to move on. It's a kind of psychological tell, a device you use to protect yourself."

"You want me to talk about Patty."

"What do you want?"

"I want Patty but I don't deserve her. You know the terrible things I was doing."

"Yes. When did that start?"

"After the baby. I...I...she was so hurt and I couldn't seem to help her. She spent a lot of time with our little nieces and my parents. That seemed to help.

"In a sense, she abandoned you. Found solace outside your relationship."

"No, no, NO! It wasn't like that. She was helping them."

"Yes, but *you* needed her. She was *your* wife."

Jimmy studied the palms of his hands. When he looked up, confusion clouded his face. He opened his mouth, closed it and shook his head. "I don't know...Are you trying to make me angry at Patty?"

"Not at all. Are you angry at her?"

"Sometimes, John, I think you are the crazy one here."

"There are no crazies here, Jimmy, just a couple of people looking for truth. I have the sense that you idealize, even idolize Patty. But, even at her best, she is human and therefore fallible, imperfect. As are you. I feel that you are carrying a shitload of buried resentment toward her. That needs to be explored before any relationship between you would have a chance. Think about it." He glanced at the clock. "Our time is up for today; see you next week."

Jimmy resisted the urge to slam the office door. *Lectured and dismissed, just like that! I'll think about whatever I want.* He walked to his car and slammed that door. "God damn that son of a bitch," he yelled as he pulled abruptly out into the traffic lane.

Funny. How we put the ones we love on pedestals. It's really dehumanizing. Marriages that survive have to let the partners fall off. Poor Kate, I loved the ideal and I fought her efforts to be real. She was up to the struggle. Eventually, I got it.. Ahh. He put the laptop away and greeted his next client.

*

Jimmy parked the car in the driveway. Inside the house, he was immersed in Patty. She had designed the room, chosen the paint and wallpaper, shopped for the furniture. He had tagged along but he left all the decisions to her.

They'd had such great plans; they had agreed to wait to have a baby until they had been married five years. So, in June 1997, Patty conceived and on March 3rd they had a beautiful daughter. She was stillborn. They baptized her Bridget as they had planned and buried her in Holy Cross with Patty's grandparents. Jimmy carefully put that memory deep and did not let himself think of it again. Now, though, the perfection of the tiny fingers and toes, the curling eyelashes, rosebud mouth and blond fuzz of her hair would not leave his vision. He could feel the solid weight of her still, little body. His own body heaved with sobs such as he could never remember. He curled up on the floor of the living room. The pent-up grief poured out.

When he woke, it was dark outside. He sat in the dark, empty house and sifted through the ashes of their dreams. Three miscarriages, in quick succession, the last one causing massive hemorrhaging and a subsequent hysterectomy. There would be no more children. They had not talked about Bridget; they did not talk about this. They went on. Communication became more and more rare. He graduated from the police academy; she got her doctorate in social work. They entertained friends, went on trips and still seemed to be the perfect couple.

Rage at John took over. "Damn you. Damn you. Damn you, John

Flynn, for raising these ghosts."
Jimmy tried to stifle the recollection.

But the memories were relentless. On 9-11, his unit got to the World Trade Center as the dust was settling after the second tower collapsed. He helped some dazed, confused, ash-covered people; he stopped a man who was trying to get into the rubble to find his wife. He watched the debris that was floating in the air and could not think what to do. He walked over to a dust-covered fire engine and put his arms around a sobbing fireman. The whole scene was beyond his ability to believe. "*This is New York for Christsake.*" All these years later and he still couldn't get his head around it.

Billy's remains had been found several weeks later and he was buried with his grandparents and Bridget. Fragments of bone, matching Meghan's DNA were not found until 2004, in a Staten Island dump. Her funeral service was perfunctory. Everyone had been through it so many times. Numbness was what Jimmy felt, only numbness.

*

Throughout the week, Jimmy was restless and unfocused. He called work and took two days off. He felt long-held ideas and beliefs crumbling. One thing he was sure of...he was angry, at God, at John, at himself but not at Patty. After all, he had shut her out of his life, not the other way around. Monday night, his mind was still going in circles. At three-twenty AM, he gave up trying to sleep and headed for the basement and the treadmill. He ran till sweat poured down his face and his body and then he ran some more. Finally, on rubbery legs, he climbed the two flights of stairs and threw himself on the bed.

A nightmare arrived promptly. He searched for Patty on a rocky beach. Wind and rain blew around him and huge waves threatened to devour the shore. He called her until his throat was sore and his voice gave out. He woke up, crying. Seconds later, he was asleep again. In this dream he was still looking for her. He stood on a cliff overlooking a river. He knew she was near but he was afraid for her. He picked his way down a rocky path to the mouth of a cave. He heard a ragged voice singing a

about five minutes late; he had never been late before. He was breathless by the time he reached the office and it took him a couple of minutes to calm himself.

John waited. After a while, he asked, quietly, "How are you? How was your week?"

Jimmy laughed, harshly. "You really are a son of a bitch, you know. My week was lousy. Just the way you set it up. I think I am losing my mind. I am a wreck, can't focus, can't sleep and had nightmares again. Different this time."

"How so?"

Jimmy looked out the window. He remembered the beach and crashing waves, the cliff and the cave and slowly related the story. "I can't believe it, John. It wasn't *only* me, it wasn't *all* my fault He was silent for several minutes. "I did try to reach Patty, after the baby was born and after the hysterectomy. I couldn't break through."

John was gentle but persistent. "How did you feel about that?"

"Hurt. Left out."

"Mmm... what else?"

"Just really, really hurt."

"That's bullshit, Jimmy. Think of your dream. What did it tell you? Patty left you, emotionally and probably sexually. Abandoned you. Call it whatever you want. Understand the circumstances, forgive her if you want to but don't deny your own feelings. For God's' sake, stop denying your feelings."

Jimmy looked away, crumpled over and held his head in his hands. "I was angry," he whispered. "I was so angry. I am still angry. I was in pain, too." His voice grew stronger, even strident. "My beautiful daughter was dead and we would have no other children and people acted as if Patty was the only one needing comfort. No one was there for me." His voice was barely audible, "I really was angry at Patty."

John wrote up his notes. *Almost there. Jimmy has finally broken through; Patty is no longer the perfect one but a real flesh and blood being. The future should be interesting.*

*

It was indeed interesting. Jimmy chipped away at the bottled up rage and began to restructure his life. For the next three months, John had little to do but watch the rapid progress he was making. He was working regularly and taking courses at Brooklyn College to complete requirements for his undergrad degree. His major was in psychology (what else, he would laugh, if you asked him). He was thinking about going to law school. He wanted to make a difference and thought that community service would give him that opportunity. He could help kids who got into trouble, maybe even keep some of them out of trouble in the first place.

A couple of weeks ago, after his usual call to Patty, he wrote her a note. "Much has changed in me since you left. I did eventually go into therapy. I wonder how you are and would love to meet and talk. Please call or write and let me know if this is possible for you." He watched for his mail eagerly and checked his phone messages obsessively. Yesterday, she called him. They were meeting tonight. Jimmy could hardly sit still as he told John. But he was disappointed in the response he got.

After a few minutes, John spoke, slowly. "Jimmy, you have worked hard for this. Take it slow. It's been a long time and Patty has

changed, too. Get to know each
other again."

Jimmy did not remember
anything else about the session.

*

They met at a little coffee shop
on Montague Street and talked until
it was closing. They walked down to
the Promenade and talked until
their teeth were chattering. Jimmy
got the car from the parking garage
and dropped Patty off at her
apartment. They met again the next
night. Within the week, they booked
a room in a posh hotel in Brooklyn
Heights. They wanted a place that

was new to both of them. Jimmy was tense to the point of nausea. *A couple of drinks would make it so much easier. Maybe, but it would be over before it began,* he thought. Patty came out of the bathroom and she also seemed uneasy. They sat in front of the electric fireplace. Neither of them had much to say. They called room service and ordered dinner but barely touched the food. Finally, Jimmy said, "We can call this whole thing off, if we aren't ready."

Patty shook her head, slowly, tears standing in her eyes. She moved closer to him and put her hand on his chest. They did not move for several long minutes. In the bed, they lay in each others' arms, talking softly until they fell asleep. They were both hungry in the morning and the breakfast was sumptuous. They showered together and toweled each other dry. Suddenly, spontaneously, they laughed and ran back to bed.

Two days later, Jimmy bounded into John's office. John laughed. "I see things are going well?"

"My God, John! It has been so long and I can't thank you enough! We have a long way to go, Patty and I, but we will be together."

They talked for the next forty minutes, tying up loose ends and then it was time to go.

Tears rose quickly in Jimmy's eyes as they shook hands. This time though, he hugged his shrink/therapist/friend, before he walked out the door.

John took out his laptop. He looked out at the ever-constant, ever-changing sky, a metaphor for his life as well as his chosen profession. He drew several deep breaths, hoping to calm his roiling emotions. He wrote up his notes, leaned back and sighed contentedly. The therapist functions as guide and goad. Jimmy had used the sessions and the intervals between them to do the hard work. He would be OK. John was grateful to have been a participant in his struggle. He checked his watch. There was time for him to do some work of his own.

His IPOD was playing *The Road is Long* by the Hollies as the guard at Greenwood waved him through the gate. John drove the serpentine road up the hill and trudged between the snow-covered headstones until he stood at his brother's grave. *"Hello, Joe. Sorry it's been so long.*

You know, I've always had a really hard time with forgiveness and yet the work I do is all about it. I've been doing some growing. A day late and a dollar short, Pop would say. I know you didn't mean to hurt me; you were both drunk and she was tantalizingly beautiful. I've had a hard time resolving my anger at your betrayal of me and then your death. I'm not there yet. Just want you to know, I'm still working on it. I love you, Bro."

He retraced his steps and started the car. The IPod continued: *He ain't heavy, he's my brother.* A tear trickled down his cheek and he chuckled at the irony of life. There are no accidents, he said to himself as he headed back to his office to meet a new client.

Juxtapositions

Joyce Webster-O'Rourke

John stood on the hill, shoulders hunched against the chilly autumn morning mist. *Here I am again, Joe. Its thirty years today and I still miss you. I know you're not here but for some reason, it's where I feel closest to you. Maybe because we got into so much trouble here (and had so much fun). Remember when you took that American history class and we sneaked in with your friend Maloney to find Boss Tweed's grave? I was scared shitless being in a cemetery in the middle of the night. Maloney laughed at me. "Runt," he whispered, "your chattering teeth will wake the dead." And then a couple of cold, dead leaves blew into his face. "Jesus, Mary and Joseph. Get me out of here," he screeched and took off like all the devils in hell were after him. He caught his jacket on the fence as he climbed over. His mother patched the coat but she grounded him for a month. We never did find Tweed's grave and I don't think Maloney came back to Greenwood until the day you were buried. He's in here now too; couple of rows over. He wrapped his car around a tree, Labor Day weekend after a party on Fire Island. I have to get to work now, Joe.*

412

Pray for me and keep an eye on Joseph; he reminds me of you, when you were nineteen, in ways that scare me.

He walked slowly back to his car. In the office, he played his messages. Two clients needing to reschedule appointments. Then: "Hi Hon, it's me. The dean of discipline at Regis called. He wants to see us, with Ciaran, Tuesday morning. He's concerned about Ciaran's attitude and schoolwork. Let me know if you can arrange it. Love you!

John sighed. *Ciaran, what the hell? He'd been moody and*

somewhat volatile lately but it's god-awful hard to know what is normal adolescent orneriness and/or behavior that requires intervention.

Four clients later, he wrote up his session notes and drove home; John really wasn't looking forward to the evening. He sometimes felt that he didn't know Ciaran, at all, anymore. The kid came and went like a shadow. Conversations were superficial. Ciaran did not initiate communication; he ignored comments that were meant to show interest and got angry when asked a direct question.

After dinner, Joseph and

Maura escaped to their rooms to study. Ciaran slumped on the couch and avoided looking at his parents. "Old Fox told me he was going to call you. He thinks I'm not working hard enough and I'm disrespectful. Then the nosy old shit had the balls to ask me if I'm 'on anything.' Can't even say the word drugs."

"Are you, son?" Kate asked quietly.

"What the hell is it with you people? You blame everything on drugs. I have other things going on."

"Look, Ciaran, we're worried about you. You seem so...so distant. When I try to reach you, you blow up or ignore me. I feel hurt but mostly, I'm frightened because this is do unlike you."

"Yeah. Well you're my father not my shrink! Just stop harassing me," he yelled. "Can I go now? I do have homework, you know."

Kate answered calmly, "OK, Ciaran," He glared at them and stomped out of the room.

*

Tuesday's weather matched John's mood perfectly. Ciaran and Kate were quiet as they waited outside the dean's office. Father Fox was a tall, stooped, aging Jesuit.

John suppressed a gasp of recognition. *How long had it been? Thirty/forty years? "Old Fox" really is old now. A ten-mile-an-hour wind would carry him away.* He led them into his sparsely furnished office and waited while they seated themselves. He smiled at John, a twinkle of amusement flashing in his eyes. "Ah, Master Flynn. It's good to see you again, all grown up and not in jail. I once had some doubts about him, Ciaran." He winked. John cringed, then chuckled as he realized he was blushing.

Father Fox went over his

lullaby. He ventured into the cave, heart pounding, and found her sitting cross-legged on the dusty floor. Her hair was wild and full of twigs and leaves, her face was streaked with mud, and her clothes were rags. In her lap she held a bundle of small branches, broken birds' eggs and dirt and she sang; *hush little baby, don't you cry.* She did not respond to him, indeed, she seemed not to see him.

Jimmy woke at ten-thirty AM. He ran to the shower and rushed through his morning routine. He had no time for breakfast. He drove as fast as he dared but was still concerns and those of Ciaran's teachers: missing homework, lateness, cut classes, poor participation and failing quizzes. When he chose, Ciaran showed flashes of brilliance. The priest asked Ciaran about home and family. "It's OK" he muttered. Then loudly:

"No. No, it's not. They don't give me any space. Always asking questions, always trying to get into my head, always wanting me to do better. Joseph can do whatever he wants and Maura is perfect."

He folded his arms across his chest and glared at his parents.

"You're feeling a lot of pressure, you don't feel accepted and you get no privacy. You're always being watched, kind of like a fish in a bowl."

"Oh yeah. You got that right.

"John, Mrs. Flynn?"

Kate was crying as she said, "We've always tried to treat them fairly. Joseph is almost five years older than Ciaran. And we try not to pry...Her voice trailed off.

John spoke softly and slowly, "Ciaran, it really hurts to see you so unhappy. What can we do to help you feel better?"

"I told you---just get off my

back. Be my father not a shrink."

"Okay," the Old Fox interjected, "channeling Cool Hand Luke, communication breaks down, fails; it's a common thing. You each mean well and you love one another but you're not hearing one another. Ciaran, I would like you and your family to see a psychologist who specializes in treating this kind of difficulty. I think you will enjoy working with him and you'll pick up some important life skills."

Ciaran did not object.

*

John's emotions were in a turmoil, as he drove to the office. He thought that Father Fox had handled things well and, professionally, he had to admire the guy's ability to blend care and humor to break through defenses. He chuckled, at the memory if his own first encounter with the austere young priest, so many years ago. He was a freshman at Fordham and failing several courses. His issues were somewhat different than Ciaran's. His father had died some years earlier; his mother was emotionally unavailable and he resented his older brother's assumed authority. Clearly, Ciaran believed that John was unavailable to him. John's feelings were conflicted; remorse that he had failed Ciaran and anger that Ciaran had rejected his attempts to help. *Failure can certainly humble one,* he mused, wryly. He punched the menu on his IPod and listened to Sinead O' Connor's lovely voice singing the Prayer of St. Francis. *Understanding, love, consolation, forgiveness of others (and of oneself)*; so easy to talk about and so hard to practice.

The day passed quickly. He finished his session notes and called Kate. She had made an appointment with Doctor Pilechowski for Thursday evening. He thought about it as he headed home and had to admit he was not wholly comfortable with it.

*

The first two clients Thursday morning were well along in therapy; a man dealing with an addiction to painkillers subsequent to back surgery and a woman going through divorce from a controlling, abusive husband.

Kelsey was a relatively new client: court-mandated due to anger management issues. She had assaulted a man who had just paid her for her services as a prostitute. The judge, citing extenuating circumstances, had ordered therapy. As often happens in such situations, her previous sessions had been sluggish and unproductive and John wondered if a working relationship could be reached. This morning, she slouched into the office, dropped two large trash bags on the floor, plopped onto the couch and put her feet on the coffee table. About thirty years old, big-busted and unkempt, Kelsey was currently homeless. She wore a semi-sheer, tight-fitting, low-cut black blouse, orange striped leggings and a cheap fragrance that failed to mask her body odor. She stared at John through large, grey, heavily mascaraed eyes. "What's up, doc?"

John stifled a laugh, he could almost see her munching a carrot. He asked her how she was feeling. "I'm okay, doc but I'll tell you straight. This isn't gonna work. I ain't gonna tell you anything when I know whatever I say goes right back to that bitch judge. I been in the system since I was ten or eleven. Been in lots of foster homes, then group homes for problem kids. Nothin' but a slave in some of them, a sex toy for men, women and bigger kids in others. I kept running away and nobody cared. Social workers, lawyers, judges, they all sucked. I got kicked out of foster care at eighteen, hitch-hiked my way east and lived on the streets ever since."   She tugged her blouse lower, eyeing John.

"Kelsey, I hear you saying that you don't trust me. Let me explain something that may help you. Yes, the judge has requested monthly reports, but, those are attendance and compliance records so that you can stay out of custody. What you talk about here is confidential, with a few exceptions."

"Yeah...like what?"

"If you threaten anyone or plan to harm yourself; things that are in some way dangerous to yourself or others, those have to be reported." He waited.

She took her feet off the table and leaned forward. Still challenging. "You know I'm a prostitute. Do you report that?"

"No, I wouldn't, but Kelsey, you know that is in your record....You can read my notes, when I write them, if it will make you feel better. I won't change them but you'll know what they say."

She stared at him for several minutes. "Y'know, doc, you might be okay. So what happens next?"

"Pretty much you talk. I listen. Maybe I comment. You talk some more. Simple but not easy. The more honest we can be, the better the results."

"So...okay...here's how I got arrested. I beat up a john...real bad. He had to go to the hospital and the cops came after me. They asked me why I hurt him and I told them it was because he said 'good girl Kelsey.' It didn't make any sense but it was what happened. He was reaching for his clothes, he smiled and said it and I went ballistic. Jumped on him, wrapped my legs around him and started scratching and clawing at him." She paused.

"Had he hurt you, Kelsey?"

"No, not at all. He was gentle, kind...he made me sure that I was satisfied, lay with me for a long time after he was done, caressed me, said he would see me again. He was a really nice guy but when he said 'good girl Kelsey' something exploded in me." She stopped, shook her head, and pressed her lips tight. She got up quickly and strode to the window. Almost inaudibly, she went on: "And I saw...kinda saw something ...remembered something. I saw...oh...so strange..."

John waited.

"Kelsey, this is a safe space. You don't need to hold anything back."

"A room...a man and a little baby. There's a woman, in a corner, behind a gate. They have no clothes on. I can't...I don't..." She covered her face and cried softly. "He was a nice man. He carried me around in a sling strapped close to his chest and he would say 'good girl Kelsey.'"

Almost ten minutes elapsed before Kelsey continued, in a choked voice. "There is a big bathtub; he takes the baby in and plays with me...oh...with her. He wrapped her in a big towel; then he rubbed sweet-smelling stuff all over her. Then he touches her in a place that makes her feel so good. My body got stiff and tight and he would laugh and say 'good girl Kelsey' and touch her over and over again." She stopped, glanced at John, waved her hands back and forth and covered her face, again. Her body heaved and she wept. When she looked up, her face was streaked with black. Still sobbing she said, "I'm scared. I can't believe this...am I crazy?"

John shook his head slowly. "Kelsey, these thoughts or memories have a cause but we don't know what it is, yet. Apparently, you were very young, a child, so whatever happened, it was not your fault. And I don't think you are crazy. You should know, though, that more of these thoughts and images may surface over time. Try not to let them frighten you. We can talk about them next week."

John reflected on Kelsey's story for a long while. *Incredible, at first, but it certainly seemed authentic as she told it. Her confusion between the baby and herself and the switching between past and present hinted at early trauma.* He pulled out the court records and read through them. She had indeed been in the system as a child and in multiple foster homes. The judge who sentenced her, on the assault charge, apparently felt she deserved a break and ordered therapy rather than jail time. He wrote up a detailed account of the session and drove home. His thoughts were focused on the up-coming meeting with Dr. Pilechowski.

*

A short, ruddy-faced man, with white hair, a well-trimmed beard, blue eyes and thick glasses,

Dr. Pilechowski shook hands with each of them. John liked him immediately. He looked at Ciaran and saw, if not trust, at least not outright hostility. *So far, so good.* Joseph and Maura seemed comfortable...another plus. Dr. Pilechowski was known for being unorthodox and his office reflected his style. It looked like a well-used rec room. A couple of shelves held games and books, a basketball was in a corner and a soccer ball had rolled under a chair. A guitar hung on the wall and a ping-pong table took up a large part of the room. There were several chairs and some over-sized pillows on the floor. John and Kate sat on chairs and the kids headed for the pillows.

"Pillowslip is a mouthful," he said, "people call me Lech, rhymes with heck. And you are Kate, John, Joseph, Ciaran and Maura. Any volunteers to start us off?" Four pairs of eyes immediately focused on Ciaran, who appeared to be studying a tassel on his pillow. "Ah," said Lech, leaning down to make eye contact with the boy. "Ciaran, you seem to be elected the family spokesperson, an important role. Or," he said, winking. "are you the 'trouble,' the one who messed up everyone's Thursday night?"

"That's me, the one who can't do anything right." And Ciaran was off, pouring out his anger, frustration and resentment at the real and imagined hurts he had endured in his family. A couple of times other family members tried to protest but Lech silenced them with a look or a wave of his hand. When Ciaran finished, he was crying. John and Kate had tears in their eyes but Joseph and Maura were indignant.

"I'm older than you, twit. I went through the same stuff when I was your age and I didn't get us all dragged off to a shrink. Suck it up," Joseph grumbled.

"Oh yeah, Mister-Great-Role-Model, you sneak out to drink with your friends and wake me up with your stinking breath at three or four in the morning. And what about the time you were so toasted you peed in the corner of our room instead of going to the bathroom? You made me clean it up. When I said I would tell, you threatened to tell Mom I did it. You think that was OK? Huh? Huh?" Joseph's face was a mask and he did not respond.

"What did *I* ever do to you?" Eleven year old Maura wanted to know.

"You never get into trouble but you're always sneaking into my room and reading my personal notes. Then you tell your silly friends and they giggle at me. I'm entitled to privacy."

He turned to John and Kate. "The two of you don't know what's going on and you blame me for everything. I'm sick of it." He looked away.

Much of what Ciaran said was a revelation to his parents. Kate said, "I'm sorry that I didn't notice what was happening. I know that's not a lot of help but it will change.

One thing we have always tried to instill in each of you is respect for the rights of others but clearly we have not gotten that across."

Ciaran gave John a challenging look and waited. Finally, John said, "I wish I had known what you were going through and how you were feeling. It was my job to know and I let you down.

Thank you for letting us know now. Your mother and I will do everything we can to help change the family interactions and make them more open and fair."

Lech said nothing but walked over to his large desk, in the corner of the room and asked Ciaran to join him. Maura trailed along. "This mobile has cut-out figures representing your family members; this one is you. Please move it gently. Don't touch any of the others. That's it. Maura, what happened when Ciaran moved his figure?"

"Everybody moved."

"Exactly. And that's what happens when someone in a family changes; everyone else has to adjust to it, to change, too. Ciaran made a major move tonight; he blew away the veils this family has been using to cover up issues none of you wanted to deal with. The biggie, of course, is Joseph's self-defeating behavior."

Turning to Joseph, all trace of lightness and humor gone, Lech observed: "That's a serious problem you have there, Joe. It runs your life and causes you to act in ways that are, at best dishonest and at worst, dangerous to yourself and to others. I believe it is a family problem?" He looked to John and Kate.

John nodded. "Almost thirty years in AA for me. My brother died in a boating accident. He was drunk.

My dad had cirrhosis; my grandmother was a binge drinker, some uncles, cousins.
Definitely a familial predisposition."

"In my family, too," Kate said.

You all have work to do. I want the five of you to meet each evening for about twenty minutes. No excuses. During these sessions you must be honest with and respectful of one another.

Then write one or two sentences summarizing your view of the family communication. Wait until Wednesday to share your writing. We'll meet Thursday." As they filed out, he put his hand on

Ciaran's shoulder and thanked him for his courage and honesty.

The ride home was quiet; only Maura spoke. "I like him."

Neither Joseph nor Ciaran disagreed.

John and Kate lay awake talking and sometimes crying. How could they have been so unseeing, so unconscious? Would Joseph be able to overcome his alcoholism; how could they help him? Ciaran had certainly taken steps to help himself and they were fairly confident he would continue to assert himself in ever more adaptive ways. Maura's behavior was not unusual for her age.

It was unacceptable in their family.
But probably easily addressed. As
he was falling asleep, a thought
floated through John's mind,
something Father Fox had said to
him, so many years ago. *"You are
human, John. That means, like
everyone else, you are imperfect,
prone to occasional errors."* It was
scant comfort.

The weekend family meetings
were bland and boring with
everyone tip-toeing around the
issues. Sunday night after ten
minutes of the usual evasions, Kate

took the gloves off. "Okay. This is ridiculous. Leck said to be respectful **and** honest. I'm not hearing any honesty. None of us is saying how he or she really feels. So let me start. I'm pissed off." She stopped as nervous laughter erupted; then she had to laugh herself. "Does someone have a comment?"

"Mom, you never say that."

"Look guys, I love you. I do everything I can to keep each of you healthy, happy and growing into the person you want to be. When I don't get any feedback, that is, honest commentary,

I'm working in the dark. And that's true in all relationships. You don't get to know another person if you don't spend some time and energy in talking together about things that matter."

For once, John kept quiet, no "shrinking" for him tonight. Kate was able to get away with things that he couldn't.

After a while, Joseph leaned forward and looked at the floor. "I know it's no excuse but...well...we're Irish. My friends are mostly Irish and they think we're supposed to drink. That's how I got started. We used to go to Central Park, sit on the wall and pass the bottle around. Once, one of the teachers caught us but he couldn't report us because he was with his boyfriend and he was afraid we would out him."

Ciaran was incredulous. "Jesus, Joseph, I can't believe you caved to all that Irish crap."

"I'm not like you, Ciaran. I was fourteen. You don't care what people think but I needed to fit in. I still do."

Joseph was crying as he spoke and Ciaran said, "I'm sorry. I never, never would have guessed."

Maura got up and hugged

Joseph.

When the meeting ended, the kids went to their rooms to write their notes. Kate and John had coffee. They sat for a long time, thinking and talking quietly. Clueless they had been, fallible they would always be but they could learn from their mistakes.

Wednesday morning, John checked his answering machine. There were the usual requests for appointments from prospective clients, and cancellations from regulars. There were also three calls from a number he did not recognize but no message. He answered the messages and made schedule adjustments. Then he called the unfamiliar number. The woman who answered did not know who had placed the calls but said that all the clients were out for the day and she was unable to give him any other information. *Probably a shelter,* he thought, and immediately thought of Kelsey. He saw a few clients, wrote up his notes and headed home.

Tonight was sharing night and he wondered what would unfold. There was some nervous chatter during dinner. Finally, Kate said, "Let's get it over with."

She and John were pretty well battered by the kids. Not enough attention, too much attention, not enough talk, too much talk. Joseph's drinking was the major concern for all. Maura's prying was discussed and Ciaran heard a good bit about his own annoying ways.

*

The New York winter set in early, almost overnight. Thursday morning wind and sleet made the roads treacherous. John left his car at home and took the train. Kelsey was huddled in the lobby of his office building when he got there. Her face was streaked with tears and her nose was running.

She was more than two hours early; the shelter emptied everyone out at eight o'clock. They went upstairs. The phone was ringing as they went into the office; he let it go to the machine while he made coffee and found some crackers. He took them out to Kelsey and told her she could stay in the waiting room until it was time for her appointment. He checked his messages. Three cancellations, due to the weather; he rescheduled them.

He took out Kelsey's court records and reread them. The story she told was supported by the meagre file. She had been found on a snowy north woods road wearing a coarse gray denim gown and men's socks that were too big for her. She had no underwear on and her body was completely devoid of hair. The only words she was able to say were "good girl Kelsey" and "no." She had been repeatedly sexually violated, starting at a very young age but was otherwise well-cared for and well-nourished. He read his session notes and was again struck by the confusion in time and identity. He put the papers away, anger, disgust and sorrow engulfing him. How could such evil exist?

After a few minutes, he called Kelsey in.

There is no trace of promiscuity or defiance in her today. Rather, she seems bewildered and frightened. "This is hard, doc. Pictures pop into my head. Hazy, blurry. I can't really see the little girl. Only the man, so big and white and the woman, with her breasts, sometimes round and sometimes hanging down. They are both smooth, no hair anywhere." Kelsey looked out the window, tears spilling from her grey, red-rimmed eyes. "I think...I think...maybe the baby...maybe ...maybe she's me."

"How do you feel when you think this?"

"It makes me cry. She shouldn't be there. She should be outside."

"Outside?"

Her voice was now a child's. "Out of that room. With people who might love her. Good girl Kelsey was never out of that room. There is a high gate and the sad woman stays there until he needs her to clean up...and he has...two things that he puts on her...she doesn't like them...they pull her breasts...I think they hurt. When he's finished, he rubs something on them and sends her back to the stool. What does it mean? Why am I there? Is it really me...the baby? Please, tell me."

"I don't know Kelsey. We can try to sort it out here but right now all we have are your memories and some sketchy court and hospital notes."

"I don't know when or where I was born or if Kelsey is my real name. They guessed at my age when they found me, called me Kelsey because that was a word I could say and made my last name Snow because I was in the snow. I am nobody to anybody."

She stared out the window for several minutes. Tears rolled down her cheeks; she made no attempt to wipe them away. Raging, racking sobs shook her body. She writhed and twisted as though she was being restrained. She jumped up, paced the room, then sell back on the couch. She curled up, pulled a pillow over her and closed her eyes.

John let her sleep while he mentally searched for options for her. *The shelter was not a safe place for her, in this vulnerable condition, and she was likely to get worse before she got better. God only knows what other horrors are lurking in her head.* He called her name several times before she responded. Telling her to wait in the outer office, he called Kate. He explained Kelsey's situation and asked if there was someplace she could stay for a week or so. Kate sighed. "John, I am a social worker...not a miracle worker. I'll get back to you."

Kelsey seemed to be asleep. He called the diner and ordered two grilled cheese and tomato sandwiches and two cups of chicken soup. Billy, the owner, said it would be about forty minutes; they were swamped with deliveries because nobody wanted to go out in the weather. Kate rang on his cell phone. "John, I spoke to Jeanne; she said they actually have a room at St. A's and she is willing to take a chance if you think it's okay. She will come by your office to pick the 'poor waif' up when she leaves work."

"Thanks, Kate. I owe you one."

"One?" She laughed as she hung up.

He woke Kelsey up when lunch was delivered. While they were eating, he explained what he had done and why. He told her that she was free to refuse. "Jeanne is a nun, she lives in a convent. They have a vacant room you can use. She knows only that you are homeless and that right now you are not safe in the shelter. You can tell her more if you want; she's a good listener. And I'd like you to come in twice a week for a while; Tuesdays and Thursdays, if that is okay for you."

Kelsey nodded and looked away. When she spoke he could hardly hear her. "There were nuns at the home...they were mean...but if you think it's okay..."

Sister Jeanne came in about one-thirty. She and Kelsey talked for a few minutes and took her bags down to the car. John wrote up his notes, made a few calls, bundled up and trudged to the train station. *Intrepid creature, that nun, really can make you believe in a good and gracious God! I can't believe she's driving on these roads.*

*

That night, on the way home from a lively session with Lech, Joseph asked if Lech would take him on as a client. "Call him," Kate and John said, in unison.

Ciaran objected. "I don't want you with me. Find your own damn therapist." Joseph was silent but

Maura jumped in. "Ciaran, you always think everything is about you but Joseph needs help more than you right now."

John and Kate shot sideways glances at each other and resolutely shut their mouths.

*

Kelsey looked relaxed when she came in on Tuesday. She wore a warm parka and a knitted hat and mittens. "I've never felt so safe, at least not since I woke up covered with hay. But it is so different. There is so much laughter and

...I...guess it's love ...in the convent, I mean. She picked up a geode and traced the swirls with her finger. Finally, she said: "I was never afraid in the room. He played with me and made me feel good. The only time he hurt me was when I was older. He held me and pushed me down onto his penis. I screamed and tried to get away but he held me there and pushed me up and down, up and down, until, all of a sudden, my whole body went stiff and then soft. He said 'good girl Kelsey' and laid me on his chest. He rubbed me until I stopped crying. Then he took me into the tub and washed me, inside, too. He put the sweet stuff all over me and put a little yellow candy in my mouth. We went to bed, the way we always did. And after a few times, it didn't hurt any more and I would run to him for him to do it. I didn't know it was wrong, doc. Oh God...I had no idea it was wrong..."

"Kelsey, what was done to you was wrong but it was not your fault. You did nothing wrong. He was a very sick individual."

"Doc, I'm still afraid I'm crazy. These pictures pop up in my head and I'm not sure they're real. The woman is all covered up now. All the little girl can see is her eyes and sometimes her red hands. She sits in the corner until he snaps his fingers; then she does what he wants and goes back to her stool. They don't talk; only he says 'good girl Kelsey' or 'Kelsey no.'" She had been dry-eyed throughout the session. Now her eyes filled with tears and she curled up in a corner of the sofa, clutching a pillow.

John waited. Sighing, he said, "Kelsey, you have uncovered many things today. Let me take them one at a time. I certainly do not think you are crazy. There is documented evidence of your having been sexually abused from a very early age. Some of the details that you 'remember' are surely altered by time and imagination. But for now, we can take them as essentially true memories of your experiences. Trust yourself.   Don't try to force memories but accept them and we can talk about them."

"John, I mean doc, the thing that most scares me is that if I saw him, now, I might run to him."

"Kelsey, this man was all you ever knew, he fed you, bathed you, played with you. He taught you to rely on him for everything, to trust him completely. He made you totally dependent; he did not even let you learn to take care of your personal needs. He groomed you to fulfill some fantasy of his own and when he had no further use for you, he abandoned you, in the bitter northwestern winter. So, yes, your feelings for him are conflicted. It may take a long time to sort them out. It's impossible to understand how a human being can do such awful things to another person, let alone a baby."

"They made fun of me, even beat me when I didn't know how to use the bathroom or clean myself. Or feed myself. Or even speak. Some of them said I was the devil's child." She shuddered, then straightened. "I don't want to talk about it anymore today...I'm happy now, sort of. The sisters are kind and good and funny. I love the singing and the prayers and all the stories about Jesus and his father and friends. Sister Jeanne is helping me read better. She made me remember the lady who taught me to speak. The lady was good to me; she told me that I was smart and pretty and she said that I would be okay. But then I got moved and I never saw her again...Sometimes I am afraid...that I will lose...lose you, too."

"Kelsey, there are no guarantees in life but I expect to be here for some years and you can come as long as you need. Our time is up for today. Have a peaceful, happy Christmas and we will meet the day after New Year's."

*

December 29. Another year winding down. John finished his traditional review of clients he had worked with over the last twelve months. He sat back and watched the pale,wintry sun struggling through the clouds and let his mind roam freely.

He thought of the fifteen year old boy whose ultra orthodox parents wanted him cured of his gayness. They came to John because they didn't want anyone in their community to know. They left, in anger, when John explained that homosexuality is an integral part of a person's identity and cannot be cured by therapy. He felt compassion for the family and frustration that he was unable to help them. *Why do I have so much trouble with perceived failures on my part? John, Y is a crooked letter. Let it be. One client, one session at a time.*

He forced himself to focus on those clients who had done well, extricating themselves from sticky entanglements, taking steps to improve their lives and/or simply coming to accept themselves as fallible human beings.

And then there's Kelsey. Easily the most puzzling client he had ever encountered. What does the future hold for her? John had no clue. She was remarkably intact, given her history. Clearly intelligent. Remarkably resilient. His peer supervision group were divided; several thought her story a colossal hoax while others thought there was substantial truth and great pathos in it. And there was some corroborating evidence. *Time will tell.*

His thoughts turned to his own family. A wry smile at the juxtaposition. Ciaran's hurt and anger had opened John's eyes to the Flynn family secrets. Joseph's alcoholism was out in the open now and he was responding well to therapy. The children s' issues had exposed fissures in the marital relationship and John and Kate had work of their own to do. *Some of that is pure pleasure!* He closed up the office, got his coat and went to meet his bride of twenty-six years in a cozy little restaurant in

Brooklyn Heights. Large, soft snowflakes drifted down and slowly transformed Brooklyn into a pristine otherworld; he caught one on the tip of his tongue. Deep joy filled him and his heart sang; he broke into a loud but somewhat off-key rendition of the Hallelujah chorus.

About the Authors

Johanna Dehler grew up in the Tyrol, the Western part of Austria. She met her husband David while on a scholarship in the US. They live with their ten-year-old daughter, Lucy, and their cat, Stampy, in Bay Ridge where they are growing deeper roots. Being a grant writer, Johanna is now venturing into more creative writing, which is a challenge she enjoys thoroughly.

Vanessa Laureano Acosta was born in Puerto Rico and came to reside in Brooklyn, New York at the age of five. She graduated from

473

Touro College with honors and a B.A. in Psychology. Vanessa has been a lover of books since an early age and began to write in her teenage years. Together with her husband, they have two beautiful daughters.

Ellen O'Rourke-Dominianni lives in Brooklyn with her family. She spends her time working, going to school, reading and writing. In May 2016, she won the Mortimer and Mimi Levitt Essay Contest for her essay on *Arrowsmith* by Sinclair Lewis.

Tom O'Rourke is married and a father of seven children and ten grandchildren. He and his wife live in Brooklyn. Tom has a B.S. from Fordham and an M.B.A. from Baruch. He published his first short novel at the age of eighty. He is now developing a short story career.

Kathy Ravalli grew up in Brooklyn, New York. She has a great mom whom she loves very much. She is very loving, and funny, and easy to talk to. She is always a good listener, talker, and storyteller. Kathy also has 3 sisters, 4 nieces, and 6 nephews. She just celebrated her 20th anniversary with her loving and funny husband whom she loves very much. Kathy has an 18-year-old loving, caring, smart, and handsome son whom she loves very much as well. Kathy enjoys cooking and baking for her family. She loves eating at nice restaurants and going to musicals with her family. Kathy also loves to write stories.

Elizabeth H. Theofan has always loved reading and writing short stories and poetry. She is retired from NYC government where she served as an Assistant Commissioner for two different agencies. After her retirement she completed a Master's degree in Biblical Studies from General Theological Seminary, which enabled her to conduct church services when her pastor is on vacation. Elizabeth has enjoyed attending six writing workshops at The Bookmark Shoppe. As a history buff, Elizabeth enjoys reading, walking tours, visiting historic sites, lectures and exhibits. If you live in Bay Ridge you have seen Elizabeth, as she walks five miles a day. Elizabeth is married to Edward Aleksey, her favorite person to enjoy exploring interesting locations with and to attend theater, movies, dinning, walks, or just relaxing at home.

Joyce Webster-O'Rourke and Tom, her husband of fifty-seven years, raised their seven children in the wonderful diversity of her beloved Brooklyn. In her "spare time," she earned her Bachelor's and Master's degrees and Certificate in School Psychology at Brooklyn College. Writing is for sharing!

35854362R00267

Made in the USA
Middletown, DE
17 October 2016